Go ahead and scream.

No one can hear you. You're no longer in the safe world you know.

You've taken a terrifying step . . .

into the darkest corners of your imagination.

You've opened the door to . . .

the NIGHTMARE room

Read all the books in
the NIGHTMARE room
series by R.L. Stine

Welcome . . .

Hello, I'm R.L. Stine. Let me introduce you to Ben Shipley. He's that boy with the dark curly hair, leaning over his computer keyboard.

Every day, Ben checks out dozens of strange websites and chatrooms. You see, he is searching for signs of alien life from outer space.

Ben's friends are worried about him. Why is he so obsessed with finding an alien? Why is he so desperate to make contact with someone from another planet? Doesn't he realize the danger he might face?

Their questions will soon be answered. Because Ben is about to meet some actual aliens . . . inside *THE NIGHTMARE ROOM*!

the NIGHTMARE room

Visitors

TO ALL ALIEN HUNTERS . . . TO ALL EARTH PEOPLE EVERYWHERE . . . A dangerous group of aliens is planning an Earth invasion sometime in the next week. REMEMBER: NOT ALL ALIENS ARE THE SAME. This group is warlike and has no regard for human life. Their most likely plan of attack: to take over human bodies. When the aliens come to your area, you will see clues. WATCH FOR THE FOLLOWING SIGNS:

    1) People you know behaving strangely

    2) Unusual lights in the sky

    3) Spontaneous amphibian replication

    4) The sudden growth of non-native plants (example: palm trees in Alaska)

5) Flashes of blue light

6) Swarms of insects out of season

I REPEAT: ALIENS WILL BE INVADING THE EARTH SOMETIME IN THE COMING WEEK. WE DON'T KNOW EXACTLY WHERE THEY WILL LAND. WATCH FOR THE SIGNS. IF YOU SEE THEM, CONTACT SOMEONE AT THE WORLD ALIEN ALLIANCE IMMEDIATELY.

Signed, Zandor

"Ben! Breakfast is ready!"

Mom's voice broke through my trance. I was sitting at my computer before school, reading a notice that had just appeared in one of my favorite chat rooms.

"Hurry up, honey!" Mom called. "You'll be late for school!"

I glanced at the message on the screen one last time. Zandor. What a wacko, I thought, switching off the computer.

My name is Ben Shipley. Why was I checking out this weird chat room? Well, you might say I'm a little obsessed. As long as I could remember, I wanted to meet an alien.

I don't think that is so weird, really, considering where my family lives—Bitter Lake, New Mexico. It's a small town near Roswell. There's a big military base in Roswell. Some of the kids at school have

2

parents who work there.

A lot of people say that aliens once landed in Roswell. I believe it.

Still, some people give us alien hunters a bad name. Like Zandor, the wacko in the chat room. "Spontaneous amphibian replication"? Like, all of a sudden there will be salamanders everywhere? Puh-leeze.

I grabbed my backpack and went downstairs for breakfast. Mom passed me on the stairs. She planted a kiss on my forehead.

"Good morning, sweetie," she cooed.

"Morning, Mom," I said, wiping her kiss off my forehead. She trotted upstairs to her room.

I love my mom, but sometimes I'm just not in the mood for her lovey-dovey stuff. She was always hugging me and my brother, Will, and telling us how much she loved us. Ecch.

In the kitchen, Dad and Will were sitting at the table, eating cereal. Biscuit, our dog, was gnawing on something under Will's chair.

"Good morning, Ben," Dad said, glancing up from his coffee. Dad is stocky, bald, and wears gold-rimmed glasses. "Sleep well?"

I nodded.

"Look, Ben!" Will yanked something out of Biscuit's mouth.

It was an old troll doll with a goofy face and long

blue hair, covered with dirt and dog drool. Biscuit had dug it up in the backyard.

Will waved the doll in my face. "Look!" he cried again. "This must be one of their babies. It's proof! Living proof, I tell you!"

Will cackled and waved the doll in the air. Biscuit, a shaggy little mutt with white and gray fur, whined, refusing to take her eyes off it.

"Biscuit wants her doll back," I told him. "Give it back to her."

Will made a weird face, flaring his nostrils and popping his blue eyes wide open. "They're in our skies!" he shouted. "They're everywhere! The aliens are coming! Ah-ha-ha-ha-ha!"

He ran out of the kitchen, laughing like a maniac. Biscuit scampered after him, still watching the doll.

"Dad, tell him to stop making fun of me," I said.

Dad frowned at me. "Ben, you know how I feel about that UFO silliness."

I sighed and shoved a spoonful of cereal into my mouth. I knew very well how Mom and Dad felt about my interest in aliens.

They didn't like it. They thought it was unhealthy and a waste of time.

But I didn't care. I knew I wasn't crazy.

I had proof that aliens had been here. Real proof. I'd found it just the day before.

But I didn't want to tell Will about it. Or my parents.

4

Will made fun of me enough already. I knew he'd never take me seriously.

I couldn't tell my parents about it, either. Every time they caught me on the computer chatting with other believers, they threatened to take the computer away from me.

So I tried to hide my obsession from them. They wouldn't have been too happy to hear about what I'd found.

Dad pushed his chair away from the table and stood up. "Well, I've got to get to work," he said. He had an office in town, selling commercial real estate. Mom worked with him part time.

He mussed my already messy brown hair. "Have a good day at school, Ben."

"Thanks, Dad." He walked to the foot of the stairs and called up to my mother. "Honey! I'm leaving!"

Biscuit trotted back into the kitchen with the troll doll in her mouth. She stopped and dropped it at my feet.

"Thanks, girl," I said, patting her. I picked up the doll and stared at it. Biscuit scampered away.

Will bounded into the room and grabbed the box of cereal.

"Checking the doll for alien markings?" he teased. He reached into the box of cereal, pulled out a handful of sweet pink O's, and stuffed them into his mouth.

"At least I don't eat like a monkey," I shot back.

"Ha ha," he fake-laughed, spitting half-chewed cereal on the table.

We were only one year apart. He was in sixth grade, I was in seventh. But we never got along very well. We were just different from each other.

We both had dark hair, but his was straight, black, and shiny. He had freckles sprinkled across his nose, which turned up at the end.

My hair was curly and coarse, and my face was pale, with no freckles. But the main difference between us, I thought, was that I was a nice guy. I didn't want to bother anyone. Will was a brat, through and through.

"Hurry up, boys." Mom swept into the room, picking up dirty dishes and dropping them into the sink.

She wore jeans and a T-shirt, and her hair was tied in a ponytail. Her hair looked so blond it was almost white. But I knew she colored it. I saw a box of hair-coloring stuff in the trash can in her bathroom once.

"Will," Mom said. "Do you have all your things together?"

Mom was always after Will to be more organized. He was basically a flake.

Not like me. Organization wasn't my problem. Just the opposite.

"Will?" Mom prodded. "Did you hear me?"

Will glanced up from the cereal box he was reading. "What? Yeah, I heard you. My backpack is upstairs."

"Well, go up and get it," Mom said. "Go on."

Will dropped the cereal box on the table and hurried upstairs. I picked up the box, neatly folded the wax-paper wrapper, closed it, and put it away in the cupboard.

"Thanks, Ben," Mom said.

I reached into my backpack and touched it—the proof I'd found the day before. Maybe I couldn't show it to Mom or Dad or Will. But I knew Summer and Jeff, my two best friends, would want to see it.

I had been trying to convince them for a long time that aliens exist. I knew it for sure. I was certain that aliens had been to Earth. They could have landed in Summer and Jeff's backyard. In anyone's backyard.

But now, at last, I had the proof I needed. And I had to show it to someone—fast.

Before the aliens attacked.

I started toward the door. But a shrill scream from upstairs stopped me in my tracks.

I froze. And heard another scream.

"Oh!" Mom's mouth dropped open. "That's Will!" she cried.

"Mom! Mom!"

Will's screams rang through the house.

I let out a frightened gasp. And led the way upstairs to see what was wrong.

We found Will in his room. Biscuit cowered in the corner, her tail tucked between her legs.

Mom grabbed Will and hugged him. "Will! What is it? What? What's the matter?"

"Murderer!" Will screamed. "Biscuit is a murderer!"

Biscuit shook guiltily in the corner.

"What are you talking about?" Mom asked. "What did she do?"

"She ate Godzilla!" Will shouted. He broke down into tears. "I caught her with her nose in the bowl!"

Godzilla was Will's pet frog. He lived in a fishbowl covered with a piece of screen.

Mom and I checked out the fishbowl. The piece of screen lay on the floor. It looked as if it has been ripped off the bowl. The frog was gone.

"Dogs don't eat frogs," Mom said. She smoothed Will's hair, trying to soothe him. "Godzilla must have escaped on his own."

Will stamped his foot. "I told you! I saw Biscuit with her nose in the bowl! She knocked the screen off. Then she ate Godzilla! Swallowed him whole!"

"Come on, honey." Mom grabbed a tissue and dried Will's tears. "You and Ben have got to get to school. Godzilla is hiding in here somewhere. I promise to look for him this morning. I'm sure that I'll find him. Okay?"

Will's teeth were clenched. His face had turned bright red. It looked as if a major tantrum might be coming on.

But my mom can be tough. Even as she cooed and soothed him, I knew Will could see in her eyes that she wasn't going to put up with much more fuss. She expected him to go to school.

He rinsed his face and grabbed his backpack. I followed him downstairs.

Mom kissed us both at the door. "Don't worry, Will. I'll find Godzilla! Have a good day at school, both of you!"

We went to the garage to get our bikes. It was January, but winter days weren't too cold in Bitter Lake. Most days I could get by with just a sweater or a jacket.

Biscuit scampered up to me, wagging her tail. I patted her. "You're not a frog-eater, are you, girl?" I said softly. "Of course not. Will is crazy."

She had that troll doll in her mouth again. She dropped it into my hand.

Alien baby, I scoffed, remembering how Will had teased me.

I know it sounds stupid. But secretly, I wished that doll *was* an alien.

I was so curious about visitors from other worlds. I knew they were out there somewhere. How could Earth be the only planet in the whole universe with intelligent life? It was impossible!

I tossed the doll back to Biscuit. Then Will and I hopped on our bikes and rode to Bitter Lake Middle School.

Will didn't talk. He was still fretting about his missing frog.

I stood up and pedaled as fast as I could. "Hey— wait up!" he called.

But I was in a hurry. School wasn't exactly my favorite place on Earth. But I kept thinking about the object in my backpack.

The proof.

I couldn't wait to show it to Summer and Jeff.

What will they say? I wondered. What will they say when I show them that aliens exist? That they have landed—right here in our town?

"Hey, look! It's Benny the Belly Button Freak!"
Rikki Mosely shouted as I pulled up in front of the
school.

"Give me a break," I muttered. I locked my bike
to the bike rack and tried to ignore her. But Rikki and
Dennis Corcoran hurried over to me.

"How's your belly button, Shipley?" Dennis said.

"Come on, Shipley. Show us your belly button!"
Rikki demanded.

"Ha-ha," I said, rolling my eyes. "You two are so
funny—remind me to laugh."

Rikki was a tall, punky girl with short, messy red
hair. She always looked kind of scuffed up. She had
a lot of holes pierced in her ears. Sometimes she

sprayed green or purple dye on her hair, just to look weird.

Dennis was husky with a dull, pudgy face. He was the kind of kid who went along with whatever someone else told him to do.

I sighed and walked up the school's front steps. Rikki and Dennis followed me. "Let's see the belly button, Shipley," Dennis said again. "We need a good laugh this morning."

"How about I show you *this* instead?" I said. I made a fist and shook it at them.

I have an outie belly button. Big deal. Most kids have innies, I have an outie.

Sometimes it pokes through my shirts a little. Otherwise, you can't see it much. Except in the summer, when I go to the community pool. Kids have been teasing me about it since I was three.

I started into the school, but Dennis grabbed me. He held me by the arms while Rikki said, "Let's see it, Shipley."

"Hey!" I cried. "Let go of me!" I struggled, but Dennis gripped my arms tightly.

Rikki lifted up my T-shirt. My belly button stuck out about half an inch. Rikki flicked it with her forefinger and said, "Boing!"

"Okay, great," I muttered. "Have you had your thrill for the day? Let me go."

"Don't you have anything better to do?" a voice

called. My two best friends, Jeff and Summer Larkin, burst through the school doors.

Summer crossed her arms over her chest and glared at Dennis and Rikki. "I mean, grow up, guys. It's just a belly button."

Dennis let me go. "We were only having a little fun, Summer," he said. His face was bright red. "Ben doesn't mind—do you, Ben?"

I rolled my eyes. Dennis had a crush on Summer, and he knew she was my friend.

"Benny is just so cute!" Rikki declared nastily. She pinched my nose, hard.

"Ow!" I cried.

"Give him a break!" Summer said.

Rikki let go of my nose. But she leaned close to me and whispered, "Watch out, Benny. Today is not your day."

I shrank away from her. She slithered inside the school building like a snake.

I admit it. Rikki scares me. She is so naturally mean. She doesn't have to think about it. Everything she does and says just comes out mean.

I rubbed my sore nose.

"Are you okay, Ben?" Jeff asked me.

I nodded. "Yeah."

"Rikki's such a jerk," Summer said. "Why does she always pick on Ben?"

Dennis shrugged. "That's just her way of kidding

around." He grinned at me. "Maybe she likes you, Ben." Laughing, he made his way into the school.

"You know what I don't like about Dennis?" Summer asked.

"Everything?" Jeff said.

Summer laughed. "Yeah. You guessed it. Everything."

I'd known Summer and Jeff since first grade. I liked Summer the minute I saw her. So I wanted to impress her. And the best way to impress a girl, my first-grade brain told me, was to shove a pea up my nose.

Summer laughed at my little stunt. Jeff thought it was gross.

Then I tried to blow the pea out—but it wouldn't budge. So Summer slapped the back of my head until it popped out, all mushy and green.

The sight made Jeff puke—all over the lunch table. Summer couldn't stop laughing.

That was six years ago. The three of us had been best friends ever since.

Summer was tall with a round face, a snub nose, pale blond hair to her shoulders, and freckles all over her face, arms, and legs. Her skin was so pale she could hardly go out in the sun without turning lobster red. But she didn't care about suntanning. Mostly she cared about field hockey, basketball, and soccer.

Jeff was her twin brother. They weren't identical,

but they looked a lot alike. Jeff wasn't quite as tall as Summer, but like her he was pale and freckly.

He wasn't nearly as athletic as she was. He liked playing video games better than sports. And he was kind of shy. Summer wasn't afraid of anybody.

The bell rang. Summer, Jeff, and I stepped inside the school and walked down the hallway toward my locker. "Five minutes till social studies."

"Wait," I said. "I've got something to show you. I found proof. Finally! Proof that aliens have landed. You—you've got to see this. It's unbelievable!"

I reached into my backpack and pulled it out. The thing I'd found in the woods the day before.

I held it up for Summer and Jeff to see. "Well?"

They stared at it and gasped. "I don't believe it!" Jeff whispered.

"You've proved it!" Summer cried. "You've really proved it this time!"

4

"You've proved that you've totally lost your mind!" Summer said.

I was holding a smooth, slightly sparkly oval-shaped white rock. It fit neatly into the palm of my hand.

Summer felt my forehead as if taking my temperature.

Jeff took the rock from me. "This has got to be the most ordinary rock I've ever seen."

"Well . . . yeah," I said. "It *looks* ordinary. But what about the tones? Don't you hear the tones?"

Summer threw a long, freckled arm around my neck. "Sure, Ben. The tones."

I stared at her and Jeff. "Are you kidding? You

really can't hear it?"

Jeff shrugged. "I don't know what you're talking about," he admitted.

I couldn't believe it. I heard a noise coming from the rock. That was what had made me pick it up in the first place.

I'd been out in the woods walking Biscuit. I started down a path I'd never explored before. And as soon as I stepped on that path, I heard a strange noise.

It was a ringing tone. Kind of like if someone hits a tuning fork, or one of those triangles they play in the school band.

I stopped and listened. Biscuit's ears perked up. She could hear it, too.

What was it? What was making that sound?

And that's when I found it. I picked it up. It was a simple-looking rock. But strange, eerie tones were pouring from it.

And I knew I wasn't imagining it because Biscuit heard it, too. She couldn't stand to have the rock too close to her head. It seemed to hurt her ears. She whined and started to paw at the dirt in a strange, crazy way.

"Stop kidding around," I said to Summer and Jeff. "Listen." I held the rock next to Summer's ear. "Don't you hear it?"

She shook her head. "Give it up, Ben."

Jeff grabbed the rock and held it to his ear. "Sorry,

Ben. It's a dumb rock. Is this some kind of joke, or what?"

Another bell rang. I opened my locker and grabbed my social studies book. I shoved the rock back into my backpack.

"I can't believe you don't hear that sound," I said. "I can hear it so clearly. Biscuit heard it, too—I swear!"

Summer tugged on my arm. "Come on, Ben— we'll be late for class."

I slammed my locker door shut and we headed for social studies. Why can't they hear it? I wondered. Is there something wrong with them?

We reached Mr. Kazaki's social studies class and stepped inside just as the final bell rang. We sat down in the back of the room.

"Today is the deadline for your term paper topics," the teacher announced. "I hope you've all decided what you'll be writing about."

He began to call on kids in the class, going alphabetically. Mr. Kazaki did everything alphabetically. Since my last name was Shipley, I always had a long wait before he got to me.

"Larkin, Jeffrey," Mr. Kazaki called out. "What's your topic?"

"The history of the Aztec Indians," Jeff answered.

"Excellent choice," Mr. Kazaki said. "Larkin, Summer?"

"The rise of women's sports in the last thirty years," Summer said.

"Good," Mr. Kazaki said. "Lester, Martin?"

My hands began to sweat as I waited. I knew what my topic was going to be. I also knew what everyone's reaction to it would be.

"Shipley, Benjamin? Your topic?"

"Alien visitors," I replied.

The class burst out laughing. Mr. Kazaki frowned.

"You did your last paper on that topic, Ben," he said. "In fact, you did your last *two* papers on that topic. You'll have to pick another topic this time."

"But I have more evidence now!" I protested. "I know I can prove that aliens have visited this planet. Just give me a chance!"

The class roared with laughter now.

A boy named Chris Miller said, "Hey, Shipley, did your mother put something funny in your cereal this morning? What a wacko!"

Summer leaped to her feet. "You take that back!" she shouted at Chris. "Ben is not a wacko! He knows what he's talking about!"

"Miss Larkin, sit down!" Mr. Kazaki shouted. "Or I'll send you out in the hall. You too, Mr. Miller."

The room began to quiet down. A few people snickered.

I could feel my face get red and hot. I sound like a lunatic, I realized. They all think I'm nuts.

"Quiet!" Mr. Kazaki slammed a book on his desk. The laughs simmered down to a few giggles.

"Ben, you have until tomorrow to find another topic for your paper," Mr. Kazaki warned. "I think you've wasted too much time with your alien quest."

I opened my social studies book and buried my face in it, fuming. What was his problem? Why couldn't I write about what I wanted to write about?

When I glanced up, I caught Summer watching me intently. I scribbled a note on a piece of scrap paper. It said, "Thanks for believing in me. You do believe me, don't you?"

When Mr. Kazaki turned away to face the board, I slipped the note to her.

She unfolded the scrap of paper and read my question. She sighed and glanced over at me. She shrugged.

I'll convince her, I thought. Somehow I'll show everyone.

At lunch, I pulled the rock from my backpack and set it down in the middle of the table. "Let's try this again," I said to Summer and Jeff.

This rock was the best clue I had ever found. I was desperate for my friends to understand what it meant.

The rock was beeping loudly. A dull, steady tone. *BEEEP BEEEP BEEEEEP.*

I pushed it across the table toward my friends. "Now do you hear it?" I asked.

The lunchroom was as noisy as always. A girl dropped her food tray, and everyone laughed and clapped. Some kids were singing an old Beatles song loudly at the next table.

But I could hear the beeping from the rock loud and clear.

Summer and Jeff stared at the rock.

"Well?" I demanded.

Before they could answer, Rikki appeared. She set down her lunch tray and snatched the rock off the table. "Where did you get this?" she demanded.

I made a grab for it. "Give it back, Rikki."

She grinned at me. "Go get it!" she cried. She tossed it across the lunchroom to Dennis.

Dennis jumped up from his table and made a one-handed catch. "Keep away!" he cried. "Keep away!"

I ran between the tables. Made a wild dive for the rock—just as Dennis heaved it to Marky Polster, one of his friends.

"Give it to me!" I shouted. "I need that!"

Marky tossed it to Maryjane Douglas. Maryjane tossed it back to Rikki.

Rikki held it in front of her, waving it at me. "Come and get it, Ben. Come on!"

The rock was ringing and beeping, making a shrill

whistling sound. Couldn't they hear it?

I leaped at Rikki. Swiped at it. She pulled it out of my reach—and heaved it out the open lunchroom window.

"NOOOO!" I wailed.

I could hear the uproar of laughter and shouts as I dove out the window after it.

I landed on my elbows and knees in the tall grass at the side of the school. Where was it? Where?

I frantically searched, pawing at the grass. I listened for the beeps and whistles.

Silence.

Moving carefully, slowly, an inch at a time, I searched everywhere. I covered every blade of grass, every chunk of dirt.

Gone.

The rock was gone. Vanished. Disappeared.

My proof was gone.

Breathing hard, sweat pouring down my forehead, I turned. And saw Rikki through the window.

She was staring out at me coldly. A strange smile on her face.

Did she know what she had just done?

I combed the grounds outside the cafeteria, but turned up nothing. My rock was gone. Totally missing.

What's wrong with me? I wondered. How did I end up being the guy that everyone picks on?

I used to have a lot of friends. But it was hard to keep my friends when I became interested in aliens.

Why did I have such a strong feeling that aliens had been to Earth? I don't know. But the older I got, the more desperate I became to find out the truth.

A few years ago, I discovered the chat rooms on the Internet. There were a lot of other believers out there like me.

Some of them were crackpots, but others had

interesting stories to tell. The more I read, the more convinced I became.

And the more eager I became to meet an alien. To communicate with someone from another planet.

And one by one, my friends started to avoid me. I understood why. But there was nothing I could do.

The only people who stayed by me were Jeff and Summer. But now even they were starting to get tired of my alien talk.

I made one last search of the ground. Then I made my way back into the building.

I had a little time left before my next class. So I grabbed my backpack and went up to the third floor, to the photography room.

Ms. Crenshaw, the photography teacher, was also a friend of mine. She was a believer, too. And she was always eager to listen to my stories about aliens.

I don't know if she believed in aliens or not. But she never made fun of me or said that I was crazy. "Maybe you'll be the first person in history to *photograph* an alien," she said.

My parents had given me a digital camera for my last birthday. I carried it with me in my backpack.

I opened the door of the photography room. Ms. Crenshaw was standing at a light table, looking at slides. She glanced up when I walked in.

She was tall and pretty young, I guess. She looked artsy, especially compared to most people in

Bitter Lake. She wore her black hair short and her lipstick very red, and lots of big, jangly jewelry.

"Hey, Ben." She smiled at me. "I was just looking at the slides from the last photo project. Yours are definitely the most interesting."

She beckoned me over to the light table. It was covered with slides that kids in my class had taken. I'd borrowed my dad's camera and taken a few shots of Biscuit. I'd posed her in front of my computer to make it look as if she were surfing the Web.

"A lot of kids took pictures of sunsets on the lake and trees in the snow," Ms. Crenshaw commented. "But your photos are really funny. They have personality."

"Thanks," I said. I reached into my backpack and pulled out my new camera. "Look what my parents gave me," I said.

"A digital camera!" She took it from me and looked it over. "You'll be able to take all kinds of cool shots with this."

She grinned at me. "Maybe you'll snap your first photo of an alien with this camera, Ben."

"Maybe," I said. And then the words burst out of me: "I found proof, Ms. Crenshaw. I know that aliens have landed."

Her smile faded. "Proof? What do you mean, Ben? What did you find?"

"I found a stone. It looked like an ordinary stone.

But it made sounds. It had to be some kind of transmitter. From outer space."

Ms. Crenshaw grabbed my arm. Her eyes widened. "Where is it?" She asked. "Show it to me."

"I—I lost it," I said.

She continued to stare at me. She let go of my arm. "If you find it, I'd love to see it. I . . . I'm very interested."

I thanked her. "Most people just think I'm crazy," I said. "You're the only one who will listen."

"I don't think you're crazy, Ben," she said softly. "But be careful, okay? Be careful who you show these things to."

The bell rang. I said good-bye and hurried to class.

All the way, her words repeated in my mind. *Be careful who you show these things to.*

What did she mean by that?

When I got home from school that day, I found Will in the kitchen with a girl his age, eating an after-school snack.

Mom wasn't home from work yet, but she always left a snack for us in the fridge. That day it was apples with some cheese and crackers.

Biscuit sat on the floor at Will's feet, licking up the crumbs he dropped.

"Hi, Will," I said, opening the fridge. "Who's your friend?"

"I'm Sophie Corcoran," the girl said with her mouth full of apple. "My brother Dennis says you're a weirdo."

Will sneered at me. "See, Ben? You're famous!"

"Can I see it?" Sophie asked. "Can I see your belly button? Dennis says it's funny."

"*Dennis* is a weirdo," I muttered.

I grabbed my apple and a plate of cheese and crackers and took them upstairs to my room. I heard Will say to Sophie, "He's going to check his messages."

"On his answering machine?" Sophie asked.

"No," Will replied. "On his *alien* machine."

Will and Sophie laughed.

I went to my room, shut the door, and sat down at my computer. I crunched on my apple and logged on to the Internet.

First I checked my e-mail. I don't know why I bothered. Hardly anyone ever e-mailed me. That day was no different—zero messages.

Then I started surfing the web, looking for new alien chat rooms. I thought I'd visited them all, but new ones popped up every day.

People wrote about UFO sightings in the sky. They wrote about aliens landing in their backyard and about hearing aliens' voices in their heads. They said they picked up signals from UFOs in the fillings in their teeth!

Some people claimed to be aliens themselves. But I could usually tell they were fakes. There was always some detail that gave them away. Like the guy who said he'd flown to Earth from Jupiter on Santa's sleigh.

I had a feeling he was making that up.

I kept hoping I'd find the jackpot—a chat room set up by *real* aliens. Where they could talk to each other, maybe from spaceship to spaceship. I'd know it if I saw it. I might not understand the language they spoke, but . . .

There were more people than usual in the chat rooms that day. I started reading some of the messages.

> Zandor's prediction is correct. I've been reading my star charts and watching the skies carefully. There is definite alien activity going on. We will see an invasion within one week—I'm sure of it. The major question is—where?
>
> —Professor George Grant

> I live in Toronto, Canada, and I've suddenly been plagued by swarms of mosquitoes. In January! It's about twenty degrees here! I know that swarms of insects out of season is one of the signs of an alien invasion. What should I do? How should I defend myself if they come here?
>
> —Mary N.

The messages in the chat room were wilder than usual. A lot of people seemed convinced that aliens were coming.

Could Zandor be right?

I thought about the space rock. If aliens have been here before, I thought, maybe they'll come back. They might be coming to Bitter Lake within a week!

I logged off the Internet and turned on my alien machine. I'd built a radio antenna the summer before and connected it to my computer.

I programmed it to send a signal out into space twenty-four hours a day. It said, "Welcome . . . welcome . . . welcome . . ."

I wasn't sure if the aliens could understand my message. And I didn't know how they would answer me if they did. Would a message appear on my e-mail? Would I hear their voices?

I also had headphones connected to my computer. The antenna brought in signals from space. Maybe the aliens would try to talk to me through the antenna! If they did, I didn't want to miss it.

I wore those headphones as much as I could. I did my homework with them on. I watched TV while wearing them. Sometimes I even slept in them. I would have worn them all day long if I could have.

But I'd been listening for months now. And so far, no aliens had contacted me. At least not in a way I could understand.

But now . . . now, maybe, I would hear from them at last.

I put the headphones on and listened. For a few minutes, I heard nothing.

Then something crackled through the

headphones. My hand froze on the mouse. I sat perfectly still, listening.

More crackling. It got louder.

Was something coming through?

It was faint at first. I strained to hear it.

It was just static. But I thought I could hear a voice far, far away. Then it stopped.

I listened harder, waiting.

The static began to clear a little. The faraway sound grew louder.

They *were* voices! Someone was talking!

A little louder. Then a little clearer. As if they were coming closer!

I began to make out a few words. The voice was high-pitched and weird.

"We are receiving signals," it said. "'Welcome . . . welcome.' Confirm Earth language."

Another high-pitched voice said, "Earth language confirmed. English. Now zooming in on location coordinates."

My heart pounded in my chest. It was happening at last!

Aliens were contacting me!

"Coordinates found," the first alien voice said. "Western Hemisphere. North America. The United States. New Mexico. Bitter Lake, New Mexico." There was a brief pause. "Fifteen seventeen Woodlawn Drive."

I couldn't breathe. That was my address!

"Coordinates set," the second alien replied. "Will now attempt contact."

I pressed the headphones to my ears, listening.

"We will land at that location in ten, nine, eight, seven . . ."

I leaped to my feet. The aliens were coming to my house! In five seconds!

I wanted to run to the window. But the cord to my headphones wouldn't reach that far. I didn't want to miss a word they said. But I didn't want to miss seeing them land in my backyard, either.

I hopped from foot to foot, too excited to think. *What should I do?*

"We have arrived," the first alien said. "I am looking at human specimen now. What a geek."

I heard the voice through my headphones—and right behind me at the same time. I whirled around.

"He's not worth the trouble," Sophie was saying

into a walkie-talkie. She was standing in my doorway, staring into my room. "Let's go to Disney World."

Will stood next to her, holding his own walkie-talkie and laughing. "You fell for it!" he cried. "You're so dumb!"

Sophie cracked up in giggles. "You're right, Will—your brother really is a weirdo!"

I should have known. Will had found a channel on his walkie-talkie that my antenna picked up. Another one of his stupid tricks.

"Beat it, brats." Summer appeared and slammed the door in their faces.

Will pounded on the door. "Hey!" he shouted. "You don't live here! You can't slam the door on me!"

Summer opened the door. Then she nodded at me. I knew just what to do.

"Well, I can!" I snarled, and I slammed the door again.

I ripped the headphones from my head and tossed them on the floor. Then I collapsed onto my bed.

"Are you okay?" Summer asked.

"Yeah." I sighed. "I don't get it, Summer. There are thousands and thousands of people in the world who believe in alien life-forms. So why don't I know any of them?"

Summer sat in my desk chair. "Most kids are into other stuff, I guess," she said. "Like sports or music. But all you ever talk about is aliens. Maybe if you had just one other interest—just one . . ."

I sat up. "Summer, I've been reading a lot of scary things lately. More and more people are saying that aliens are coming to Earth—soon. Really soon. I think they might be coming here."

Summer sighed. "Ben, you need another hobby." She climbed to her feet. "I've got to go home now and do my homework. But after dinner I'm going to come over and pull you out of this room. I'll bring Jeff if I can tear him away from the TV."

"Okay. See you later."

She opened the door and spotted Will and Sophie huddled in the hallway.

"Why don't you two get a life?" she snapped. I heard her stomp downstairs and out the front door.

A few minutes later, Mom's car pulled into the driveway. She poked her head into my room and saw me lying on my bed. "Ben, what are you doing? Don't you feel well?"

"I'm okay," I replied.

"Why don't you go outside and take a walk or something?" she suggested. "It's a nice day, and you need more fresh air. I worry about you, always sitting at that computer day and night—"

"Mom—" I protested.

"It's not healthy," she went on.

"I don't feel like walking," I said.

She frowned, and I knew that look on her face.

She can be very stubborn when she wants to be.

She opened the door wider and stalked over to the bed. She pressed her hand on my forehead.

"You're not sick, so I want you up," she ordered. She grabbed me by the arm and pulled me to a sitting position. "Why don't you go outside and ride your bike or something?"

"I've got homework to do," I whined. That's usually the ultimate weapon—homework. But she wasn't buying it.

"How about a short walk? Breathe in a little fresh air. Take your sweater." She snatched up a green sweater I'd dropped on the floor a few days earlier. "Come on, Ben. It will do you good."

She pushed me out the door. I heard Will and Sophie giggle as I walked past Will's room.

I stopped in the kitchen for another apple. "Come on, Biscuit!" I called. "We're going for a walk—whether we like it or not."

Biscuit scampered to the back door. I opened it and she burst outside, running and jumping happily.

Once we left the backyard and got deeper into the woods, I began to relax. I hated to admit it, but Mom was right. It felt kind of good to get outside for a little while.

Biscuit ran ahead of me, yapping like an excited puppy. I realized we probably didn't take her on walks as much as we should have. We usually just let her out into the yard.

Biscuit kept trotting along, and I followed her, not paying much attention to where I was going. I walked and walked, deeper into the woods than I'd ever gone before. I wasn't just following Biscuit anymore. Something seemed to be pulling me along.

I kept thinking about the trick Will and Sophie had played on me. For a few minutes I'd really thought aliens were contacting me. It had been so exciting.

Just because Will played a trick on me doesn't mean I'm wrong, I thought. There are still aliens out there somewhere. I know it for sure.

Biscuit stopped a few yards ahead of me and started barking like crazy.

"What is it, girl?" I asked, running a little to catch up with her. *Maybe she's spotted a rabbit or something,* I thought. But Biscuit wasn't exactly a hunting dog. She usually didn't even get excited about cats.

Biscuit ran a little farther ahead, still barking. I chased after her. I found myself in a big clearing. I stopped dead in my tracks. And stared in amazement.

In the clearing, a huge, perfect figure eight was burned into the grass. Biscuit ran along the edge of it, sniffing every inch of it.

The figure was big enough to fit a small house

inside it. And it was absolutely, perfectly shaped.

A human could never make such a perfect figure eight in the grass, I thought.

I'd never seen anything like it before.

I walked up to the figure eight and stepped inside one of its loops.

Zap! A shock jolted through my body. I stared at my hands.

They were glowing!

The electricity surged through my body. My arms and legs shook. My whole body shuddered.

"Ohhhhhhh."

Pain shot up and down my body as jolt after jolt crackled through me.

Make it stop! I begged. Make it stop!

With a struggle I heaved myself outside the loop. Gasping for breath, I collapsed on the grass.

The electric jolts had stopped. But my body still shook and my skin tingled.

I held my hands in front of my face and stared at them. I wasn't glowing anymore.

But when I'd stepped inside the figure eight . . .

What does it mean? I wondered.

I was sure of only one thing. This was more proof that aliens had been there. There was some kind of weird force inside that figure eight—an unearthly, inhuman force.

I've got to get a picture of it, I decided.

"Come on, Biscuit!" I called. I began to run back

home. Biscuit scurried after me. We raced all the way through the woods until we reached my backyard.

I paused outside the back door, panting. I was so excited, I couldn't wait to tell someone about the figure eight.

I was tempted to tell Mom. But I was afraid to because I knew she'd only worry. And I couldn't tell Will. He was too . . . Willish.

No, I thought. I'll have to keep it a secret until Summer and Jeff come over tonight.

In the meantime, I had to get my camera.

I passed through the kitchen on my way to my room. "Dinner's almost ready," Mom said. Dad was setting the kitchen table.

"I've just got to run back into the woods for a minute," I said. "There's . . . uh . . . something I want to take a picture of."

Mom and Dad exchanged glances.

"Something in the woods?" Dad said. "Since when do you do nature photography?

"Uh . . . well . . ."

Mom set a casserole dish on the table. She frowned at me. "Sorry, Ben. It's time to eat. You can go back out after dinner."

"But, Mom—" I protested. "It's important! It will take only a minute or two."

Mom and Dad looked at each other again. Their expressions were strange, troubled.

"Ben, you heard your mother," Dad said. "It can wait until later."

No, it can't, I thought. It will be too dark to take a photograph after dinner.

"Will!" Mom called upstairs. "Dinner!"

"Sit down, Ben," Dad said.

Frustrated, I sat down while Mom spooned macaroni onto my plate. I was dying to get a picture of that figure eight. What if it disappeared before I could get back there?

"What are we having?" Will asked as he bounded into the room and slid into his chair. "Not tuna casserole again?"

"Macaroni and cheese," Mom told him, loading up his plate. "Eat some salad, too."

She and Dad sat at the table and started eating. I picked at my food, wishing dinner would hurry up and be over.

I might as well wait for Summer and Jeff to get here now, I thought. It's going to be too dark. But at least I can take them into the woods and show them the figure eight.

We ate in silence. It seemed a little strange to me. Usually Mom and Dad asked us all about school and everything. But that night they were strangely quiet.

Finally, Dad said, "Your mother and I have to go out tonight. Just for a short while. We'll be back by nine."

"Mrs. Jenkins will be next door if you need anything," Mom added.

"Where are you going?" Will asked.

"No place special," Dad replied. "We should be back by nine."

I glanced at Will. He shrugged. I could tell he was thinking what I was thinking—what's up with them?

"I'm going to hang with Jeff and Summer tonight," I told them. "They're coming over later."

"That's fine," Mom said. "Keep an eye on Will."

"I'm going with you," Will said to me. "Wherever you're going."

"Yeah. Sure," I muttered.

No way was he coming to the woods with us.

When dinner was over, Mom and Dad left the dirty dishes in the sink, which was also strange. They always cleaned up right after dinner.

Mom got her purse. She and Dad drove off.

"Where do you think they went?" Will asked.

"Who knows?" I replied.

"Maybe they're going to surprise us with something," Will said.

"Maybe," I said, but I doubted it.

I logged on to my computer while I waited for Summer and Jeff to arrive. I wanted to see if I could find any information about weird figure eights. Instead, I ended up on a website with this message:

Spontaneous amphibian replication is a well-documented sign of alien invasion. Amphibian earth creatures such as frogs, salamanders, newts, and certain lizards reproduce extremely quickly in the presence of alien life-forms. . . .

"Turn that thing off!" I glanced up to see Jeff and Summer standing in the doorway. I rushed over to them.

"You guys, I've got something so amazing to show you!" I hung my camera around my neck, grabbed them both by the arm, and dragged them downstairs.

"Hello, it's nice to see you. Thank you for coming over . . ." Jeff teased. "There are dozens of greetings you could have used, Ben."

"Where are you taking us?" Summer asked.

"Just follow me," I told them. "You've got to see this for yourselves."

I led them outside. It was a beautiful, clear night. I paused in the backyard to gaze up at the sky. There were millions of stars and planets.

Which ones had aliens living on them? Which ones had sent visitors to Earth?

We flicked on our flashlights and started into the woods. There was no wind that night. Everything was very still.

"It's kind of spooky out here," Jeff whispered.

We walked for about ten minutes. I hoped I could

find my way back to the figure eight. What if I couldn't? Jeff and Summer would never believe anything I had to say then.

"How much farther?" Summer asked. "It feels like we've been walking forever."

"Are you sure you know how to get back?" Jeff asked.

"We won't get lost," I promised. "I think we're almost there."

A few minutes later, I stepped into the clearing.

There was the figure eight. The moon had risen, and the figure seemed to glow in the moonlight.

"This is it," I told them. Even though it was dark, I lifted my camera and snapped a few pictures.

Summer and Jeff stared at it. Summer rolled her eyes. "Here we go again," she mumbled. Then she turned to me.

"This is it?" she echoed. "What's it?"

"The figure eight!" I cried. "Look it at! It's huge! Something burned it into the grass!"

Summer and Jeff stepped closer. "So?" Summer said.

"Don't you think it's mysterious?" I cried. "I mean, how did it get here? Who made it? Why?"

"It's just smushed-down grass," Jeff said.

"Step inside it!" I dared them. "Just step over that line. You'll see."

"You go first," Jeff said to Summer.

"Wimp," Summer muttered. She stepped across the line in the grass and stood inside one of the loops of the eight.

I waited for her body to jolt the way mine had.

But she just stood there calmly.

"Come on in, Jeff," she said. "There's nothing to be afraid of."

Jeff stepped inside the loop. Nothing happened to him, either.

"Don't you feel anything?" I asked them. "Don't you feel the power?"

"Ben, stop it," Summer pleaded. "You're really scaring me."

"Look!" I moved carefully toward the figure eight. I hesitated because I wasn't eager to get shocked again.

I stepped quickly over the line.

Zzzip!

I felt a sharp shock and jumped right back out.

"Did you see that?" I demanded.

"I saw you jump," Jeff said. "But I already knew you could do that."

"You don't feel a shock or anything?" I cried.

"Ben, is this supposed to be another alien thing?" Summer asked.

"Well—"

"All you think about is aliens," Jeff said. "You see signs of them everywhere!"

"Face it. You're obsessed," Summer said. She paused and looked me straight in the eye. "Ben, you're starting to sound really crazy."

My jaw fell open. "How can you say that?" I asked. "You guys are my best friends!"

They exchanged that look again. My heart sank. If I couldn't count on Summer and Jeff, who could I count on? I was beginning to feel so alone.

Then I heard something. A rustle.

I glanced up at the treetops. The air was dead calm. Not a breath of wind.

I froze, listening. Something rustled again.

"Did you hear that?" I whispered.

"Now what?" Summer said. "Are the aliens landing?"

"Shhh!" I held one hand up to shush her. We all stood still.

Behind us, a twig snapped. I heard feet shuffling through the leaves.

"*Now* did you hear something?" I whispered.

Summer and Jeff nodded.

There was someone else in the woods!

I ran toward the sound. Whoever was out there, I was going to catch him—or her, or it.

"Ben, what are you doing?" Summer called. She and Jeff hurried after me.

I dashed into the woods. I heard footsteps running away from me, back toward my house.

The moonlight filtered through the tall trees. I flipped on my flashlight. I stopped for a second to listen.

Someone was running to my left. I ran in that direction, my flashlight beaming.

I was getting closer. I could hear the person breathing heavily.

"Who's there?" I called.

No one answered.

At last I got close enough to catch a glimpse. The beam of my flashlight grazed the back of the person's head.

I saw a flash of blue. Bright blue. A glowing bright blue.

A roaring boom—like thunder—made me gasp.

An alien!

It was finally happening. I was chasing an alien!

"Come back!" I shouted. "I just want to talk to you! I won't hurt you!"

The flash of blue vanished behind a clump of tall bushes.

"Please—come back!"

I dove into the bushes. My feet tangled in a long, twisting vine.

With a cry, I fell to the ground.

My heart thudding I scrambled quickly to my feet. I searched for the eerie, blue color. Listened for footsteps.

No. The alien had disappeared.

Summer and Jeff caught up with me. "Did you see that? A flash of blue!"

They shook their heads. "We heard someone running," Summer said. "But we didn't see anyone."

"But did you hear that boom?" I went on. "It sounded like thunder. And look! It's perfectly clear tonight. There are no clouds in the sky!"

"Calm down, Ben," Jeff said. "Maybe it was a sonic boom from one of those new jets at the military base in Roswell."

"Maybe," I replied. "But the flash of blue light—it's one of the signs."

"Signs of what?" Summer asked. "Of Ben Shipley losing his mind?"

"One of the signs of alien life," I said. "I'm not crazy, you two. First that weird figure eight. Then the flash of blue . . ."

They started back toward the house. My mind spinning, I hurried to keep up with them.

Summer and Jeff didn't say much. I could tell I was freaking them out.

I'm not losing my mind, I thought. I know I'm right.

I saw an alien tonight. It *had* to be an alien!

Summer and Jeff said good-bye and hurried home. I felt bad. They were the only two friends I had left. But I was beginning to wonder how much longer they'd put up with me.

Will was in his room, playing video games. I logged on to the computer and checked my e-mail.

For once, I had an e-mail message.
I opened it. It was from Zandor. It said:

All signs point to an alien invasion this week. Location still unknown. Do not forget to watch for the signs. Read them over again. Memorize them. If you see any of the signs, you'll know the aliens are coming to your area.

These aliens are not friendly. They will harm you. Be careful.

—Zandor

Why is he writing to me? I wondered. Was this a mass mailing—or was he trying to contact me?

I thought about the warning signs. So far I'd seen only one—the flash of blue light.

I yawned. I was beginning to feel sleepy. I glanced at the clock.

It was almost nine-thirty. Mom and Dad weren't home yet.

That's strange, I thought. They said they'd be home by nine. They're almost never late. I wonder where they went, anyway.

About an hour later, at ten-thirty, I finally heard a car pull into the driveway. I got up and glanced into Will's room. He was asleep.

I went downstairs. Mom always had a smile for me. But now her mouth was set in a grim line. Dad was frowning pretty intensely, too.

"Where've you guys been?" I asked.

"Nowhere really," Mom said softly.

"Did you go shopping or something?" I asked.

"Ask a lot of questions—don't you, Ben?" Dad snapped.

I shrank back. What was his problem?

I sat down on the steps and watched them as they loaded the dinner dishes into the dishwasher.

"Um—is everything okay?" I asked.

"Fine," Dad answered through gritted teeth. "Everything's just perfect."

What's up with them? I wondered. They're acting so weird.

"Ben, do me a favor. Go to bed," Dad barked.

"But I usually stay up until eleven," I protested.

Mom whirled around to face me. "Don't argue with your father."

"Okay, okay," I said, standing up. "I'm going to bed."

"And no Internet surfing!" Dad said.

I stumbled up the steps and went into my room. I left the door open a crack. I was hoping to hear them say something that would tell me what the matter was. But they didn't speak at all.

Weird. Weird. Weird.

A few minutes later, I saw Mom walk past my room. Maybe she'll tell me what's wrong, I thought. If I just ask her nicely enough.

I crept into the hallway. Mom wasn't in her room.

Where did she go? I wondered.

Then I noticed that the door to the attic was open a crack.

That's strange, I thought. Why would she go up there? Dad always kept the attic door locked. He said the floor wasn't finished and it was dangerous to go up there.

We never use the attic. Why did Mom go up there tonight?

I opened the door and crept up the stairs. Near the top, I stopped.

Whoa. There's a room up there, I saw. Dad lied. It's completely furnished. And the floor isn't unfinished. It looks perfectly solid.

Why did Dad lie? Why?

Squinting into the dim light, I spotted Mom. She was standing with her back to me. She pulled open a closet door.

Slowly . . . slowly . . .

And as the door opened, a glow of light poured out from the closet.

A blue glow.

I gasped. And stared in amazement at the eerie light pulsing out of the closet.

I saw it for only a second.

Someone behind me grabbed my shoulder, hard. Mom slammed the closet shut.

I spun around—and stared up at my dad.

"Ben, what are you doing up here?" he demanded.

"Uh . . . what are *you* doing up here?" I shot back.

"Nothing you'd be interested in," Dad said sternly.

"We're just fixing the attic up a bit," Mom said.

"It . . . it was going to be a surprise for you," Dad added.

I could tell he was lying.

Why were they both acting so strange? Why

wouldn't they tell me the truth?

"I saw a blue light," I said. I pointed.

Mom shook her head. "Light? I didn't see it."

"Must have been a reflection from the street," Dad said. "Now, go to bed, Ben. It's really late."

I wanted to ask more questions. But I could see it was no use. I said good night and hurried back to my room.

I knew I wouldn't be able to get to sleep.

I stared out my window for a long time, watching the sky.

I was dying to find out what they were doing in the attic. And I wanted to see what was inside that attic closet.

Maybe tomorrow when they're not around, I thought.

I fell asleep at last. In my dreams I saw an army of aliens, slimy and reptilian. They were seven feet tall, walked on two legs, and were covered with wet scales. There were thousands of them, marching around and around in a figure eight.

I stood at the center of the eight, where the two loops intersected. The aliens began to march in a spiral, moving closer and closer to me. . . .

I held up my hand. They stopped. "Do not fear me," I said. My voice came out loud and booming. "I am your friend. Speak to me. Show me your language."

The lead alien stepped forward. "On our planet, we greet each other this way."

He stuck out his tongue. It was a long, slimy tongue, maybe five feet long.

He tickled me with it. Then he licked my face.

I didn't like it. But I didn't want to make them angry. So I said nothing.

"Now," the alien leader said. "You must touch my hand. That means you accept our greeting."

I reached out and touched his wet, slimy hand. It felt as if it were covered in mucus.

I shivered. It was disgusting. But I had to do it for the good of interstellar relations.

Wait a minute, I thought. My hand really *is* touching something slimy and wet.

Am I still dreaming? Am I still asleep?

I touched the slimy skin again.

Okay, I thought. I'm definitely awake.

I opened my eyes.

And started screaming.

It wasn't a dream.

I bolted upright. I was in my room. In bed. Moonlight poured in through my window.

My hand was wrapped around a slimy creature.

With a cry, I opened my hand. The creature plopped onto the floor.

A frog.

"Whoa!" I whispered. Godzilla. My brother's frog.

"You're alive!" I whispered. I knew this would make Will really happy.

I reached down and gently picked up the frog. "Where have you been hiding, boy?" I climbed out of bed and started toward Will's room.

But my foot landed on something wet.

I glanced down—and saw that I was standing on

another fat, green frog.

"Huh?" I leaped back. Stumbled into my dresser.

Two frogs stared up at me from the dresser top. Another frog hopped over my foot.

"Hey!" I turned and saw that my bed was full of frogs now. Fat, dark creatures hopping wetly over my sheets, over my pillow.

"Get out!" I cried. I swiped the two frogs off the dresser. One of them clung to my pajama sleeve.

I felt a wet, slimy frog moving up one leg. Another one clung tightly to the back of my neck.

"Help!" I screamed. "Mom! Dad!"

And as I screamed, I remembered . . . remembered the warning . . . one of Zandor's warning signs!

Spontaneous amphibian replication.

It was happening—right in my room!

Frogs! Dozens of frogs everywhere!

I batted one off my head. Tugged one from under my pajama sleeve.

"Mom! Dad! Hurry!"

I couldn't move. I couldn't take a step without squashing a frog.

Suddenly, they began moving in one direction. Toward the wall. No. Toward the window.

I gaped in amazement as they hopped over the rug, off the bed, off the furniture. They made their way to the open window. A dark, plopping stampede.

And then out the window. They poured out the window as if swept by a wave.

My bedroom door swung open. The ceiling light flashed on.

"Mom! Dad! Look!" I cried. "Look!"

Blinking, tying their robe belts around them, they gazed around my room. Finally, Mom stared at a creature beside my foot.

"You found Godzilla!" she exclaimed. "Ben, that's great!"

"But—but—but—" I sputtered.

I gazed around my room, empty now. Only one frog, puffing up and down at my feet.

"There were hundreds!" I cried. "Hundreds!"

"Another bad dream?" Dad asked.

"At least you found Godzilla," Mom said. She bent down and picked him up. "I'll take him to Will's room. Go back to sleep, Ben."

"Try not to dream," Dad said as they closed the door behind them.

I dropped onto my bed. The sheets still felt slimy and wet from all the frogs.

This was it, I realized. Another warning sign. It's all over the Internet that aliens are coming this week.

And so far, I've seen two of Zandor's signs. The blue flash. And the amphibians.

And one other sign, I realized. People acting strangely. Like Mom and Dad up in the attic.

I sat on my bed and pulled the covers up to my neck, staring out the window.

The aliens are invading any day now, I realized. Warlike aliens. And they're coming here.

They're definitely coming here.

I've got to warn everyone. Somehow, I've got to make people believe me!

And I've got to find out the truth about Mom and Dad.

I'm going back up to the attic, I decided.

I'm going back up there tomorrow.

I hurried home after school.

Will was in his room with his friend Sophie Corcoran. They were on the floor in front of the TV, playing PlayStation games.

Mom and Dad weren't home.

"What's up?" I called to Will as I passed his room.

He and Sophie didn't even turn around. Too busy with their game.

Good, I thought. They won't see me snooping around in the attic. So they won't tell Mom and Dad.

I made my way down the hall. Once again, I pictured Mom and Dad up there, acting so strange, so tense and frightened.

And I pictured the flash of blue light from the attic closet.

They were so eager to get me out of there, I remembered. So desperate for me not to see what they were doing.

They even lied to me.

Why?

I stopped at the end of the hall. I grabbed the knob on the attic door. I started to turn it—then stopped.

"Hey—" I cried out.

The door—it was locked by a heavy steel padlock.

Now I felt more confused than ever.

Why would Mom and Dad do that? What were they trying to hide from me?

I didn't have a clue.

A few minutes later, I was sitting at my computer with my headphones on, trying to find Zandor.

I wanted to tell him that I was seeing the warning signs of an alien invasion. I needed to ask him what I should do.

I contacted the World Alien Alliance. *I am looking for Zandor,* I wrote. *I have seen several signs of the alien invasion, including spontaneous amphibian replication. If anyone knows what I should do, please answer.*

"Ben! Open this door!"

I quickly switched off my computer monitor. I didn't want Mom and Dad to find out what I was doing. I knew they'd try to stop me.

I got up and unlocked the door.

"It's open," I called as I sat back down at my desk.

Mom and Dad opened the door and stepped into my room. Dad cleared his throat. "Ben, what are you doing locked up in here?" he asked.

"Nothing," I said. "Just—um—listening to some music." I tapped my headphones.

"Ben, your father and I are worried about you," Mom said. "Your teacher called. Mr. Kazaki. He told us that you insist on writing papers about aliens even when he's asked you not to."

"You know how we feel about that, Ben," Dad said. His usually mild-mannered face looked puckered and tense. "We don't like this obsession of yours."

"I know," I said.

"We think it would be best if you just stopped it," Mom said. "Find something else to do. No more aliens!"

"Okay, sure." I was just trying to get them to leave me alone. I stared at their faces, hard and tense.

Was it just worry? Or was it something else?

"No more aliens," Dad said sternly. "No more

talk about aliens. No more searching for aliens. Just drop it. Drop it."

"Do we understand each other?" Mom added.

I nodded. "I guess."

"Good." They turned and made their way downstairs, leaving the door open. I stood up and closed it behind them.

Why were they doing this?

All sorts of crazy ideas whirred through my head.

Did they know something about the alien invasion? Were they afraid of what they knew? Were they trying to protect me?

Yes, I decided. They were probably trying to keep me safe.

But why couldn't they be honest about it?

I switched my monitor back on. A light blinked on my screen.

"Whoa." I had an e-mail message.

> We are here. We're looking for you.
> We don't know who you are yet.
> But we will find you.

I stared at the message, my whole body shaking. Who could have sent it?

The aliens?

Why would they be looking for me?

I'd dreamed of this for years. But now I was terrified.

This e-mail could be a joke, I thought. Some jerk in the chat room could have sent it. Or some kid at school. Anyone could have sent it.

Still. A chill ran through me as I stared at the message.

Someone knocked at my door. I quickly switched the monitor off again.

"Come in," I called.

Summer threw open the door and walked in. "Get your shoes on!" she said. "We're going ice-skating."

"Excuse me?"

"The new ice rink is supposed to be really cool, and a whole bunch of kids are going."

"Summer, listen to me." I grabbed both her shoulders and looked her straight in the eye. "An alien invasion is coming. The aliens are already here! I know it for sure now—"

Summer clapped a hand over my mouth. "You listen to me," she said. "I would like to spend just one afternoon without talking about little green men. Okay?"

She lifted her hand off my mouth. "But I have proof—" I insisted.

She rolled her eyes. "I've seen your proof."

"But—"

"I'm serious," she said. "You can tell me whatever it is you have to say after we go skating. But I can't stand much more of this. It's—it's getting harder and harder to be friends with you, Ben."

My mouth fell open, but I didn't try to say anything. Was she saying she wouldn't be friends with me anymore if I kept talking about aliens?

I needed her. If the aliens were here, I needed a friend. I couldn't afford to lose her and Jeff.

"All right," I agreed. "I have something very important to tell you. But I will wait until after skating."

She grinned. "What a relief. Let's go."

I threw on my sneakers and a jacket and followed her outside.

We rode our bikes through my neighborhood and out onto Route 13, leading downtown. We passed a new development of adobe houses, then a strip mall.

Something caught my eye on the side of the road. A small bush I'd never noticed before.

I pulled over and stopped, staring at the plant.

"Have you ever noticed a plant like this around here before?" I asked Summer.

"No. But then, I'm not exactly into plants."

I wasn't *sure* what it was, but it looked a lot like holly—that stuff you see all over Christmas cards. It had large red berries growing inside pointy green leaves.

One of the signs of alien invasion was the sudden growth of non-native plants. Was this holly plant native to New Mexico? How come I'd never seen one like it?

"Are we going to stand here, staring at that bush all day, or what?" Summer said.

"It's just that—never mind." She'd never believe that a bush could be proof of alien life. I mounted my bike and started pedaling toward town.

We turned off Route 13 onto Main Street. The downtown area of Bitter Lake was really small. Main

Street was about seven blocks long, lined with shops that had been there since the fifties. A drugstore, a grocery store, a diner, a gift shop . . .

We rode through town. The new ice rink stood at the very end of Main Street, where it intersected with the highway. It was called the Ice Castle.

It was huge and white, built to look like a castle. The outside was lit up with colored lights, even though it was daytime. And it was packed with kids.

"Where's Jeff?" I asked.

"Home playing video games," Summer replied. "You know him. He doesn't like sports much. Except for pro wrestling."

I knew what she meant. I wasn't crazy about sports myself. I didn't even like wrestling.

"I haven't been ice-skating in a couple of years," I admitted. "I might be a little klutzy."

"You'll be fine," Summer said. "It's like riding a bike."

We rented ice skates. Then she led me onto the ice. People zipped past me, skating to the beat of the dance music.

I stepped onto the ice, wobbling a little. My ankles felt loose, kind of weak. But soon I was skating smoothly.

Summer zipped around the rink, skating forward, backward, and sideways. I just stuck to plain old straight ahead.

In the center of the rink I spotted Dennis Corcoran. I braced myself for another belly-button assault. But he just smiled and waved at me. Everyone was having such a good time skating, they forgot to tease me.

Then, through the crowd of skaters, I spotted a flash of blue hair. Who was that?

The blue-haired girl turned around. Rikki Mosely.

I grabbed Summer as she whizzed past me. "Look who's here," I whispered, nodding at Rikki.

"Check out her hair," Summer whispered back. "Can you believe she colored it blue? And those clothes . . ."

Rikki was wearing a neon-green-striped shirt with orange-and-white-checked pants. They clashed with her blue hair.

But I didn't care about her clothes. I was wondering about that thing I'd glimpsed in the woods. That flash of blue.

Could it have been Rikki? Could the flash of blue have been her hair in the beam of my flashlight?

Summer grabbed my wrist. "Come on, Ben. Let's skate."

I took another turn around the rink. But I kept glancing at Rikki. She was skating alone in the center of the ice.

Something else was bothering me about her.

I watched her as she skated, keeping her eyes on

the ice. She skated around and around by herself, first on one skate, then on another. She looked as if she were trying to draw something on the ice with her skate. Trying to draw a very particular figure.

"Look!" I said to Summer. "Look at the way she's skating. She's making the exact same shape as that burn mark we saw in the woods!"

"Yeah," Summer said, rolling her eyes. "It's called a figure eight. All figure skaters do it!"

"Maybe so," I said. "But nobody else in this rink is making a figure eight. Only Rikki."

Summer shook her head and skated away. I leaned against the wall, studying Rikki.

She's always hated me, I thought as I watched her skate that figure eight over and over. I never understood why.

Summer skidded to a stop and stared at me. "Earth to Ben. What are you thinking?" she asked.

"It could have been Rikki spying on us in the woods," I murmured, more to myself than to Summer. "If so, why did she run away from us? What was she doing at that figure eight in the first place?"

"Ben—you said you'd give it a rest," Summer scolded.

But I couldn't. The more I thought about Rikki, the more questions I had.

I had to find out if she ran from me in the woods that night. I started across the rink toward Rikki.

"Ben? What are you doing?" Summer demanded. She chased after me. But nothing could stop me. I was too excited.

I skated up to Rikki, stopping her in the middle of one of her figures.

"Rikki—was it you? Was it you in the woods?" I cried.

"Get out of my way," she snarled.

"Tell the truth," I demanded. "Why were you there? Why did you run?"

"I don't know what you're talking about," she said. She straightened up tall and glared at me. "Now get out of my way!"

"Not until you admit the truth!" I cried. And then the words just slipped out of my mouth. Crazy words. A crazy idea.

But maybe not so crazy. "You're an alien, right? I'm right, aren't I?" I said.

Rikki's eyes narrowed. She skated a step closer to me, threateningly. "Have you totally lost it? Are you going completely mental, Shipley?"

I knew I sounded crazy. But it was too late. Too late. I had already asked the question. No way I could take it back.

And what if I were right?

And now I was so excited, I didn't know *what* I was saying! "Please—I want to be friends," I said. "I don't want to stop you in your mission. I just want to learn about it. I want to know about your home planet and your people."

"You're really asking for it, Shipley," Rikki said. She shoved me, hard. I fell backward, but some guy caught me before I fell. He pushed me back up to my feet. I stood there for a second, wobbling.

All the kids on the rink gathered around. One kid started shouting, "Fight! Fight! Fight!" Soon the others joined in.

Rikki charged at me and threw a swing at my head. I ducked. It missed me.

"Fight! Fight! Fight!" the crowd roared.

She grabbed the collar of my jacket and yanked me close. We teetered on the ice, face-to-face.

Her breath smelled sour, like rotting food.

And then it happened. Her brown, cat-shaped eyes changed. They morphed into burning, glowing *bright blue spheres*.

"Sssssstay away from me," she hissed. It wasn't her normal voice. No girl had a voice like that.

It was the rattling hiss of a monster.

I'm right! I realized, staring at those glowing blue eyes, that twisted, evil face.

I'm right—she's an alien!

My last thought before everything went black.

I opened my eyes. My head ached. I was lying on my back. I could feel the cold, wet ice through my shirt and pants.

I gazed up. Kids had gathered around me, staring down at me. I squinted, trying to focus. I felt so groggy. The rink seemed to be spinning around me.

"Where is she?" I murmured. "Where did she go?"

The faces jutted toward me. I stared at them but I couldn't make out who anyone was. A girl loomed over me.

I struggled to sit up. But my head felt heavy. I couldn't move.

"Ben? Are you okay?"

My vision slowly cleared. Rikki stood over me. "You're okay?" she repeated.

"Wh-what happened?" I choked out.

"You slipped," she said. "I was kidding around with you. And you slipped and hit your head. You were knocked out."

I stared up at her. My mind was still spinning. Did I imagine the whole thing? Her glowing eyes? Her inhuman, rasping voice?

It had all seemed so real . . . so terrifying.

"Glad you're okay," Rikki said. She faded into the crowd of kids.

Summer appeared.

I blinked up at her. I lifted my head and shook it a little, squeezing my eyes shut.

After a minute I felt better. Summer grabbed me by the arms and helped me sit up. My head didn't feel so heavy anymore. My mind began to clear.

As the kids began to realize that I was all right and they probably wouldn't get to see any blood, they began to skate away.

"Summer—did you see Rikki's glowing eyes?" I asked. "Did you hear what she said to me?"

"Ben, you just hit your head. Let me help you up."

She helped me to my feet and we skated over to the side of the rink. I dropped limply onto a bench.

"Summer, her eyes changed," I cried. "They

turned blue, and they glowed with an eerie light! And she hissed at me in a totally different voice! Did you see it? Didn't anyone else see it?"

Summer dropped her head in her hands. "Ben, when are you going to give up on this? Rikki is not an alien. She's just a weirdo who likes to give you a hard time!"

I sighed. I shook my head again. It still hurt a little.

Am I going crazy? I wondered.

"You hit your head pretty hard," Summer said. "I think you'd better go home. I'll go with you."

We unlaced our skates and turned them in. It felt funny to walk in shoes again.

"Do you feel well enough to ride home?" Summer asked as we unlocked our bikes.

"I feel perfectly fine," I insisted, and it was true.

We rode home. Summer didn't say much. Every once in a while she glanced over at me. I think she was checking to make sure I hadn't gone completely nuts.

I'm not nuts, I thought. The fresh air had cleared my mind.

I had seen so many of the warning signs. Too many warning signs to ignore.

Maybe Rikki isn't an alien from outer space, I thought. Instead, maybe she's been *invaded* by an alien. *Possessed.*

I'd seen it plenty of times in the movies and on TV. Aliens didn't always take over a planet using lasers and explosions. Sometimes they just took control of people's bodies, instead!

What if aliens landed in the woods? Their spaceship burned that figure eight in the grass. They spread out through our town. And they are invading us one by one!

Maybe Rikki is the first. Maybe others have been possessed. Maybe the aliens have come to possess all of us!

"What are you thinking about?" Summer asked.

"Uh . . . nothing," I muttered.

"I'll call you later," she said as we skidded to a stop in front of my house. "Bye!"

"Bye." I waved and parked my bike in the garage. I went inside the house.

"Mom?" I called. "Dad?"

No answer. I walked into the kitchen. Through the window I spotted Mom and Dad sitting out back on the patio.

That's strange, I thought. They never sit outside like that in the winter.

It wasn't exactly freezing out—maybe fifty or sixty degrees. Winter days weren't too cold in Bitter Lake. But still, it wasn't exactly balmy, either.

The kitchen window was open a crack. I could hear their voices faintly.

I strained to listen. I could pick out a few phrases here and there.

"Getting in the way . . ." Dad said. "We can't let him find out the truth. . . ."

". . . never wanted him to know . . ." Mom said. "Never wanted . . ."

". . . the home planet . . ."

I gasped. Huh? The home planet!

No, I thought. Oh, no!

Could I be right?

Had the aliens invaded? Had they possessed Rikki?

And my own parents?

I remembered the blue flash of light in the attic. How alarmed my parents were when I followed them up there.

The padlock on the attic door.

My own parents? My own parents?

I swallowed hard. I realized my whole body was trembling.

Did this mean that Will and I weren't safe?

Suddenly, as if she sensed my presence, Mom turned around.

"Ben!" she said. "You're home."

They stood up quickly. They looked really tense, as if they were hiding something.

They slid open the back door and came inside. "We'll have dinner in about an hour," Mom told me.

"Uh . . . okay," I said. I stared at them. They *looked* the same. But I knew they weren't.

I have to reach Zandor, I thought. I have to tell Zandor what is happening here.

"I'm going up to my room now," I said.

I grabbed a soda and hurried upstairs. My bedroom door was closed. I opened it—and gasped in horror.

My room had been completely trashed.

The bed was torn apart. Clothes had been pulled out of my drawers and tossed over the floor. The closet door stood open, clothes, shoes, and games spilling out of it. Someone had pulled all the books off my shelves and tossed them everywhere.

"I don't believe this!" I groaned.

I stepped inside the room and gazed around. My posters had been torn from the walls. They lay in shreds on the floor.

The floor was so littered with stuff, I couldn't walk through my room without stepping on something. I spotted something metal on the floor next to the computer. I stepped over and picked it up.

My alien antenna! Someone had completely wrecked it! It was twisted, broken, and bent all out of shape.

Then I noticed something. The computer screen was glowing. My computer was on. When I'd left to go skating, I'd turned it off.

I stared at the monitor. Someone had left a message on the screen.

Just two sentences.

Two sentences . . .

> We don't want to be discovered.
> This is your only warning.

My heart pounded as I stared at the message on my computer screen.

I read the words over and over.

Who could have done this?

Trembling, I tore through my things until I found my digital camera. I tried to take a photo of the screen. But all that came out were wiggly lines.

"Ben?" I heard Mom and Dad coming down the hall toward my room. They stopped in the doorway and cried out in shock.

"Oh, my goodness!" Mom shrieked.

"What on earth happened in here?" Dad cried.

"I—I'm not sure," I told them.

As they stepped into the room, the message on

my monitor fizzled. Then it disappeared.

Dad crossed the room and stood in front of the window. "Ben—did you leave this window open all day?"

"Uh . . . yeah," I replied. "Do you think . . . a burglar did this?"

"Is anything missing?" Mom asked.

Dad didn't give me a chance to answer. "I'm calling the police," he said.

"Is anything missing?" Officer Fleming, a tall, skinny young policeman, repeated Mom's question. He was kicking through all the stuff on the floor of my room, investigating the break-in.

"No," I said. "I don't think so."

"Ben, why would someone do this to you?" Dad demanded. "Could it have been one of the kids you know at school? Maybe some kind of prank?"

Finally, I couldn't hold it in any longer. "This wasn't a burglary," I said. "This was a warning. There was a warning on my computer screen when I walked in here."

Officer Fleming stared at the screen, which was blank. "What kind of warning?" he asked.

"It said, 'We don't want to be discovered. This is your only warning.'"

Officer Fleming squinted at me. "Do you know who left the message?"

"No, not really," I admitted, "but—"

"Do you use your computer a lot?" the officer asked me. "I mean, do you talk with strangers in chat rooms and such?"

I glanced at my parents, who were glaring at me.

"Well . . ." I began. "Yes. You see, there have been warning signs about an alien invasion."

I stared at Mom and Dad. Would they react to that?

They stared back at me sternly. Dad frowned and shook his head.

Officer Fleming raised his eyebrows and turned to my parents. "So you talk to people in those UFO chat rooms, Ben? How many times a week?"

"Every day," I admitted.

"Ben!" Dad shouted. "You promised us you had stopped that!"

"What kind of people have you been talking to?" Mom asked. "Ben, did you ever give anyone our address?"

"No!" I insisted. "Nobody from a chat room broke in here. It was an alien! The aliens are here. They're trying to scare me away!"

"Calm down, son," Officer Fleming said.

"How can I be calm?" I cried. "The aliens have landed. I know they have. They're going to take everybody over. We've got to stop them!"

Officer Fleming sighed as if he'd heard all this too

many times before. "You know, being so close to Roswell has this effect on some people," he said to my parents. "I'll keep an eye on the house. Let me know if any more evidence comes up."

"Thank you, Officer," Mom said. She led him downstairs.

Dad glared angrily at me. "Ben, you know how we feel about you and those chat rooms. I had no idea you were spending so much time on them."

Mom returned. "I'm very disappointed in you," she said.

"I'm afraid we'll have to punish you," Dad said. "You're grounded for the rest of the weekend."

"Dad!" I cried. "You can't do that! I've got important things to do!"

"Sorry," he muttered. He and Mom left the room. They shut the door behind them.

Grounded! My parents had never grounded me before.

This proves it, I thought.

This proves that aliens have possessed Mom and Dad.

Maybe the big alien invasion is this weekend. And that's why they want to keep me in my room. So I can't warn anyone about it.

I'm not staying in here, I decided.

I have to get out. I have to warn people. I have to let everyone know the danger we are all in.

Where should I start? Where could I get the proof I needed to show everyone that I was right?

Suddenly I knew. I knew who I had to see. The last person I'd ever go and visit.

Rikki Mosely.

I grabbed my camera and locked my bedroom door. Then I climbed out the window and onto the trellis.

Halfway down the trellis, I remembered Rikki's frightening eyes and voice at the rink. I almost climbed right back into my room.

No, I told myself. Swallow your fear. You've got to do this. You've got to save the town. You've got to save your friends.

I jumped quietly onto the grass. Then I climbed on my bike and rode to Rikki's house.

Rikki's house was a small one-story ranch house at the edge of an older development. Her neighborhood had been built across the woods from mine. It was kind of run-down.

Luckily, there were a lot of trees and bushes around, and a lot of cars parked in the street, so I had plenty of places to hide. I left my bike behind a hedge and crouched beside a white van to watch Rikki's house.

A man in a dirty white T-shirt came out of the house. He had long sideburns and his belly stuck out over the top of his jeans.

That must be her father, I thought.

He grabbed a garden hose and turned on the water. He stood in the yard for a few minutes, watering some plants near the house.

Then Rikki appeared. She wasn't dressed as strangely as usual—just jeans, a flannel shirt, and white sneakers.

I watched her walk around to the side of the house. What's she going to do back there? I wondered.

A few seconds later she returned, walking a girl's bike with a banana seat. She jumped on her bike, waved to her father, and pedaled off down the street.

Perfect, I thought. Now I'll see what she's up to.

I hurried to my bike and followed after her, careful to keep a safe distance away. She headed toward town.

She pedaled down Main Street and stopped in front of a row of shops. She chained her bike to a parking meter and went inside the grocery store.

I locked my bike a block away. I crept up to the grocery store and stared through the window. What was she buying? What did aliens eat, anyway?

A few minutes later, she came out of the grocery store with a plastic bag in her hand. I pressed myself flat against the wall. She didn't notice me.

She turned left and headed down the street. Very carefully, I followed her, keeping about a block behind her. She ducked into a plant shop.

Interesting, I thought. What does she need from the plant store?

I crept up to the shop door. I could see her inside, talking to the clerk. The clerk nodded and walked into a room behind the shop.

Rikki waited until he was out of sight. Then she reached into a bag of fertilizer.

She grabbed a handful of it and stuffed it into her mouth.

Oh, wow! I thought. She's eating fertilizer!

Is that what the aliens eat?

Hungrily, she reached into the bag for another handful.

I raised my camera to the window to snap a picture.

At that moment, she turned toward the window.

I tried to duck down. Too late.

Did she see me?

Her eyes flared, bright blue again. A blinding flash of blue, bright as laser light.

Did she see me?

Did she?

My heart thudding in my chest, I hurried around the corner and plastered myself against the wall of the building.

I heard the front door of the plant store open and shut. I peeked around the corner.

Rikki came out of the store carrying a small bag of fertilizer. She glanced to the left and the right. I shrank back against the wall.

And waited.

Waited holding my breath.

Finally, I let my breath out in a long whoosh. I peered around the corner again.

Rikki was unlocking her bike. She mounted it and rode away down the street.

Whew, I thought. That was a close one.

"What are you doing?" a voice called sharply.

I whirled around. Summer and Jeff were standing behind me, eating ice cream cones.

"Oh, wow. I'm so glad to see you two!" I cried breathlessly. "You guys—you have to listen to me. It's not about warning signs and musical rocks anymore. This is real. The aliens are here! You've got to help me! They're invading the planet. They're going to take over everything!"

Jeff glanced at his sister. "Should we say something?"

Summer nodded. "You're getting too weird, Ben," she said. "I'm so sick of hearing about aliens, I could scream. I can't take it anymore."

"No, please—" I turned to Jeff.

"You'll help me, right, Jeff?" I asked. "You believe me, don't you?"

Jeff shook his head. "I'm sorry, Ben," he said. "I've got to agree with Summer. I'm tired of talking about aliens. It's not right. You need help. Really."

"No!" I cried. "You don't understand! If you'd only listen to me—"

Summer shook her head. "Give it a rest, Ben. Call us when you get over your alien thing."

They turned and walked away down the street, licking their ice cream cones.

I couldn't believe it. My last two friends. The only two people who had stuck up for me all along. And now they were telling me to forget all about it.

What's going on? I wondered. Everyone is abandoning me! Just when I need help the most.

Well, they'll be sorry they ever doubted me, I thought. All I need is a picture of Rikki eating fertilizer or doing something weird. If I can show them that, they'll change their minds. They've got to.

But for now I'm on my own. I've got to prove that aliens are here.

And I've got to do it alone.

I stared at the people I passed as I rode my bike home. If the aliens are invading, any one of them could be possessed, I realized. And I wouldn't know it.

No one would know it.

I passed a man sitting in his yard, pulling up clumps of grass. Was he eating the grass?

I blinked.

Did I just see him eat a handful of grass?

A car pulled up next to me when I stopped for a red light. A little girl in the backseat pressed her face against the window and glared at me. Then her eyes changed just as Rikki's had! They grew big and bright and flashed bright blue!

I almost fell off my bike. The girl laughed at me as the light changed and the car pulled away.

Did that just happen? I wondered. Was it real, or did I imagine it?

No. It was real.

These things I'm seeing—they're all real.

The aliens *are* invading, I realized.
And they're everywhere.

On Sunday, my parents took Will to a hockey game. I sneaked out of the house once again.

I rode my bike around town. The farther I rode, the more terrified I became.

I saw people sitting on their front lawns, eating clumps of grass and dirt. People on the street gazed at me with flashing blue eyes.

A group of kids hissed at me as I rode by. They hissed and giggled and rolled on their backs in a puddle of wet mud.

Finally, my legs were shaking too hard to pedal my bike. I climbed off and walked it home, leaning on it for support.

The aliens are everywhere, I saw. Everywhere.

Somehow they have possessed nearly everyone in town.

Am I all alone now? Am I truly the only one not possessed?

I can't be, I decided. There are still people like me who can be rescued—if they find out the truth in time.

Who could I talk to? I had no friends left.

Suddenly, I thought of Ms. Crenshaw. The only teacher who never laughed at me about aliens. The only teacher who encouraged me, who was nice to me.

Ms. Crenshaw. Was she my last hope?

On Monday morning, I rode as fast as I could to school. I locked my bike and ran straight to the photography room.

The lights were out. Ms. Crenshaw must not be in yet, I decided.

At the back of the classroom, Ms. Crenshaw had a big darkroom. I knocked, to make sure she wasn't in there developing photos.

No one answered, so I opened the door.

I flicked on the light.

"Oh, no!" I cried. "Oh, no!"

I couldn't believe my eyes. I blinked to make sure they were working okay.

I stared at a wall of metal cages. Dozens and dozens of cages.

And inside the cages . . .

. . . inside them . . .

Creatures! Weird-looking creatures! Living creatures!

What were they?

I had no idea. But one thing I knew for sure.

Those creatures were not from Earth.

Trembling, I stepped into the long room. The metal cages were stacked one on top of the other, lining every wall.

My eyes moved from cage to cage. Inside each cage sat an egg-shaped thing, covered with fur, about the size of a tennis ball.

Eggs, I thought. Eggs with thick fur.

The furry eggs had three blue eyes and small jagged mouths that drooled a greenish slime. They didn't seem to have any arms or legs.

My stomach churned. I struggled to breathe.

What were these things? Were they alien *food*?

The furry eggs clapped their mouths open and shut, making tiny squeaking noises. Like baby birds.

In a corner I spotted a larger, golden cage. The brown egg-shaped thing inside that cage was bigger than the others—a little bigger than a softball.

It pulsed with energy. Its fur glowed with a strange blue light. It opened its mouth, and I saw bigger, sharper teeth than the others. It drooled a constant flow of blue slime onto the bottom of its cage.

The pulsing blue light reached out through the cages to the smaller eggs. They all seemed to lean toward it the way plants lean toward the sun.

Are they feeding on it? I wondered.

I stood frozen in the darkroom, gazing at these creatures in amazement. For so long, I had wanted to meet an alien. It was my dream, my obsession.

But now that I was finally staring at alien creatures, I felt only terror.

I started to back up to the door. Then I gasped when I heard voices outside—in the photography room.

Who is it?

I have to hide!

But where?

I glanced around the darkroom, searching for a hiding place. I saw a door at the far wall. I yanked open a door—and discovered a small bathroom.

I heard footsteps. Someone was about to enter the darkroom.

No time! I squeezed into the bathroom and silently pulled the door, leaving it open just a crack.

I hid behind the door, peeking through the crack.

A second later, I recognized Rikki's voice. "We don't have much time," she said. "Come and see for yourselves."

Who was she talking to?

"We'll do whatever we can to help," a boy said. That voice sounds very familiar, I thought.

Rikki walked into the room and sat down. Two other kids followed her.

At first I couldn't see them clearly. It seemed to be a boy and a girl. They both had light blond hair.

"We need a plan," Rikki said. "We need to work fast."

"Ben Shipley should be next," a girl said. "I'm tired of his spying. He is a big troublemaker."

"Yes, Ben should definitely be next," the boy agreed.

I nearly choked. My breath caught in my throat.

What did they mean? Why were they talking about me? Who *were* they?

Then the girl turned toward the bathroom door. And I could see her face clearly.

Oh, no, I thought.

Not you. They haven't gotten to you, too!

Sitting next to Rikki I saw Summer and Jeff.

Summer walked along the room, studying the weird, egg-shaped things in their cages.

"They look weak," she said.

Rikki nodded. "They won't survive much longer. They need human hosts."

My mind spun.

The egg creatures—they weren't alien food. *They were the aliens!*

But they needed to be inside humans to survive on earth.

I pressed myself against the door and listened hard.

I saw Jeff studying the bigger egg in the golden cage. "But what about the leader?"

"He is keeping the others alive," Rikki explained. "He is keeping us *all* alive."

"But he cannot continue if the others do not find human hosts," Summer said. "We have only a day or two to find them hosts."

I couldn't believe it. I felt so dizzy I could barely keep on my feet.

Summer and Jeff! They were helping Rikki and the aliens! They were *possessed* by the aliens!

And all along they'd been telling me I was crazy! Telling me to forget my alien obsession.

Where is Ms. Crenshaw? I wondered. Does she know that they are using her darkroom to hide the aliens?

"There are dozens of aliens here," Jeff said. "How can we find that many hosts so fast?"

"Think about it," Rikki said. "That's why we're keeping them here at the school. We have hundreds of healthy young host bodies here. We just need to figure out a way to get the aliens inside the students."

"Don't worry, my brothers and sisters," Summer cooed to the furry eggs. "We won't let you die. We'll find a nice host body for every one of you—just like mine."

"And mine," Jeff added.

"And mine," Rikki echoed.

It took all my strength not to scream out at that moment. I wanted to scream. I wanted to run. To push right past them. To leap out into the hall and warn the other kids to escape—before it was too late.

But before I could move, the darkroom door opened and Ms. Crenshaw walked in.

Thank goodness, I thought. She'll see what they are doing. She'll stop them!

But no.

"How are they doing?" Ms. Crenshaw asked.

"They're weakening," Rikki said.

"We must take care of that quickly," Ms. Crenshaw said. "We don't want the mission to fail."

Ms. Crenshaw . . . my last hope. She was an alien, too!

"We must find host bodies. And we must find The One," Ms. Crenshaw said.

The One?

Who was she talking about? One of the aliens?

The alien leader?

Find *The One*?

I shut my eyes, my brain spinning.

The warnings had been true. These egg-shaped aliens had invaded earth. And each one needed a host body.

Ms. Crenshaw, Rikki, Summer, and Jeff were already host bodies to aliens. And they had a plan.

They were going to plant the others inside the kids at school!

I've got to stop them! I thought. I can't let them get away with this!

I've got to get out of here and warn everyone! I realized.

But for now I was stuck in the bathroom.

And that's when Jeff said the words I dreaded most.

"My host body ate something sticky for breakfast," he said. "I've got to wash my hands."

I backed away from the bathroom door as Jeff moved toward it. There was no place to hide in here. Just a sink and a toilet.

I flattened myself against the wall behind the door. I knew it was hopeless. If Jeff pushed the door open, it would hit me. He'd have to be an idiot not to notice me.

I swallowed hard. What if they catch me? What will they do to me?

Jeff pushed open the door. The bottom of the door bumped against my sneakers and bounced back at Jeff.

He peeked around the door.

He saw me.

I was trapped.

I smiled meekly and gave him a little wave.

He wasn't happy to see me.

"Ben!" he growled. He grabbed me by the arm and dragged me out of the bathroom.

"He's been spying on us!" Jeff cried.

Rikki glared at me. "You pain! I warned you to stay away! What are you doing here?"

"Summer!" I cried. "You're not really one of them—are you?"

Summer nodded. "Don't be afraid. It is your fate."

I tried to back away, but there was no room.

"Don't be afraid," Ms. Crenshaw repeated. "It doesn't take long."

"One day, all earthlings will host our kind," Rikki

said. "You are powerless against me."

"You'll never get away with this!" I cried. "I'll do whatever I have to do to stop you!"

"Oh, no, you won't," Rikki said. "Because you're next."

I started to run for the door.

Rikki and Jeff grabbed me. Rikki pushed me into a chair. She, Jeff, and Ms. Crenshaw kept me pinned there while I squirmed.

Summer opened one of the cages. She carefully took out a round, furry alien.

"What are you doing?" I screamed, struggling to get away. "Let me go! Let me out of here!"

Summer carried the alien to me.

"How can you do this?" I wailed. "Summer—it's me! Ben! You've known me since first grade! Remember? Remember how we met? At lunchtime?"

"I have no idea what you're talking about," Summer said. "Now be quiet!"

She lifted the furry egg toward me.

It isn't really Summer, I realized. An alien has taken over her mind and body.

Jeff reached for my mouth. "Noooo!" I screamed. He pried my jaw open.

"Okay," Rikki said to Summer. "Shove it in."

I tried to scream. I tried to pull away.

But they held me tightly in place.

Summer held the furry egg in front of my face.

I stared at the green drool running down the creature's furry front. Its three eyes stared at me, not blinking, not moving.

The whole creature throbbed excitedly. Its thick fur bristled.

Then Summer shoved it into my mouth.

I struggled and squirmed, trying to escape. I tried to clamp my mouth shut, but Jeff held it firmly open.

I shot my tongue forward, trying to push the horrible creature away.

But Summer pushed hard and crammed it farther into my mouth.

I gagged as the fur bristled in my mouth. Summer pushed it deeper.

I gagged again. The fur scratched the back of my throat.

Summer gave it another shove. My mouth was filled now.

The egg squirmed. I choked. I couldn't breathe. A sour slime trickled down my throat.

Summer gave the alien one final push.

"HUNNNNNNNNNNGGGH!" I gagged as it slid down my throat.

Jeff let go of me. I swallowed.

I could taste the sour slime on my throat. Could still feel the bristly fur filling my mouth.

The alien slid down to my stomach.

It was inside me.

I coughed and gagged again.

Ms. Crenshaw walked to the bathroom and returned with a paper cup of water. "Drink this," she ordered. "It will help."

I drank the water. It helped clear my mouth and throat a little.

Rikki let go of me. I jumped to my feet, dazed and frightened. I could feel the alien inside me, moving in my stomach.

I've got to get rid of it, I thought. I've got to get it out of me as soon as possible!

I stuck my fingers down my throat and tried to vomit the alien up. Nothing happened.

Rikki laughed. "Once we are inside of you, you can't get rid of us."

"That can't be true," I said, and tried to vomit it up again. It wouldn't budge.

Instead, a strange feeling surged through my body. It felt like electric waves rising from my stomach—to my brain.

"You will feel strange at first," Summer told me. "But you'll get used to it."

"The alien inside you connects you to the leader," Jeff explained, pointing to the biggest egg. "Soon you will feel his magnificent energy."

I did feel something. It wasn't magnificent, but it was powerful.

I felt wave after wave. And then I heard a voice. A voice deep inside me.

"You are my host body now," it said. *"You will receive my thought waves. You will do all you can to protect me."*

My own brain struggled against this. No! I thought. I'll fight you! I'll fight you!

But I could feel the alien's power growing stronger and stronger.

"I tried to warn you not to meddle with our plans," Jeff told me. "When Summer took you skating, I trashed your room. I left that message on your computer to frighten you."

"And we sent you that e-mail, warning you to stay away," Summer said. "But it doesn't matter now."

"You're free to go," Rikki told me. "Now that you have one of us inside you, there's nothing you can do to stop us. You are on our side now. You will help us."

"You can help us tomorrow," Summer said.

"Tomorrow?" I choked out. "What is happening tomorrow?"

"You'll see," Rikki replied. A cold smile spread over her face. "Tomorrow will be a wonderful day."

"But—but—" I sputtered. "Tell me. Tell me about tomorrow."

"Go home," Jeff said. "You are one of us now."

"Yes," the alien voice inside me said. I could feel it getting stronger, louder, taking over my brain. *"You are one of us now. You will follow our wishes. And you can't do anything to stop it.*

"You are powerless," the voice roared inside my head. *"Powerless."*

I hurried out of the darkroom, through the photography room, and into the hall. The halls were empty. Classes had started.

I didn't bother going to class. I ran outside, climbed on my bike, and pedaled for home. Leaning forward, gripping the handlebars for dear life, I fought the waves of alien energy that surged through me.

I've got to tell someone, I thought desperately. Mom and Dad?

Can I trust them?

Or have they swallowed aliens, too?

But then I felt my brain arguing with me. *"It's not a horrible thing. It's wonderful thing. You are a hero. You are saving an alien life."*

Oof! A sharp pain stabbed my stomach. I tried to keep pedaling, but the pain forced me to stop.

I bent over, clutching my stomach.

"What are you doing to me?" the voice demanded. *"Stop! I order you to stop causing me pain!"*

Huh? I'm not doing anything, I thought.

After a short while, the pain eased up. I continued on my way home.

Hurry! I told myself. Hurry!

But to my horror, my body began to slow down. I struggled to pedal faster, but I couldn't.

I leaped off my bicycle. A sharp stab of pain shot through my stomach again. I crouched down, moaning, rolling on the ground and holding my stomach.

"What are you doing to me?" the voice called. *"You are not allowed to cause me pain."*

"I—I'm not doing anything!" I cried out loud.

"You are not cooperating!" the voice boomed. *"I will make you pay for that!"*

Somehow I made it home. I staggered into the kitchen. Mom and Dad were still home, cleaning up the breakfast dishes.

"Ben! What are you doing home?" Mom demanded.

I can't tell them, I decided.

I can't trust them.

"I'm not feeling well," I said. "The nurse sent me home sick."

I felt another stab of pain. *"You must suffer the way you are making me suffer!"* the voice inside me boomed.

I suddenly felt so weak.

"You do look pale," Dad said. "Why don't you go upstairs and lie down?"

"Good idea," I said. Holding my breath, I walked upstairs to my room. Another sharp pain seized my stomach again. I collapsed on the bed.

What is this pain? I wondered. Why is the alien doing this to me?

I lay huddled on the bed as the pain grew sharper, so intense I could barely breathe.

I'm . . . dying, I realized. And suddenly, I knew it was true.

I was dying! Disappearing.

I was vanishing as the alien came to life inside me.

I writhed and moaned in pain, struggling against it with all my might.

The pain moved to my head, pounding, throbbing. Worse than any headache I'd ever had. Pain so intense I couldn't see.

I'm going crazy! I thought. I'm going to die! To disappear inside this pain.

Have to fight it. Have to fight it . . .

And then, deep inside me, I heard a horrifying *snap*!

At that moment, I knew what had happened to me.

The alien inside me had taken over.

I had fought the alien—and lost.

I felt as if I were floating. I didn't know if my eyes were open or closed, but I couldn't see anything.

Everything went very still.

Then I felt my chest move up and down. I'm breathing, I realized.

I opened my eyes. I stared at the ceiling above me. The ceiling of my room.

My room. Was the alien controlling my thoughts now? Or could I think whatever I wanted? I decided to test it.

The aliens must be destroyed!

I have to fight them however I can!

"Hey!" I cried out.

That was *me* thinking! Not an alien!

I sat up. I had a heavy feeling in my stomach. As if I had eaten too much.

I tried to sense the alien's energy, his thoughts, the waves of power he had spread through my body.

No. Gone. The pain was gone. All that was left was the weight in the pit of my stomach.

What happened? I wondered. Did the alien die?

I looked up. Mom and Dad were staring at me from the doorway.

"Ben—what's wrong?" Mom asked, hurrying into the room. "How do you feel?"

"We heard you talking to yourself," Dad said. "We were worried—"

"The aliens," I blurted out. "I was right. The aliens have come. They've landed and—and—"

I stopped.

A chill of fear ran down my back.

What was I saying? Why was I telling *them*?

I had seen the blue glow in the attic. And I had overheard their conversation about the "home planet."

I knew I couldn't trust them.

They both stood over the bed, staring down at me. Gripped with fear, I watched for their eyes to flash bright blue.

"Ben, we have to tell you something," Mom said.

"Yes. This is the right time to tell you," Dad whispered.

Oh, no, I thought. This is it.

This is where I learn the horrifying truth about my parents.

I realized I was holding my breath. I let it out in a long, shuddering whoosh.

"What? What is it you want to tell me?" I choked out.

Mom sighed, a sad sigh. "We have to tell you the truth, Ben," she said. "The time has come."

"You know, you've been obsessed with aliens since you were very small," Mom said. "You've always been desperate to contact an alien visitor."

"I know that. So?" I demanded eagerly.

"Well, we know the reason. We know why you're so interested in beings from other planets," Mom said.

Dad grabbed my shoulder. He stared deep into my eyes. "You've always been interested in aliens," he said, "because *you* are an alien!"

"I—*I'm* an alien?" I whispered. I started to laugh. "Is this a joke?"

"No joke, Ben," Dad said, his eyes still locked on mine.

"Mom, Dad—you don't understand," I said. "I just saw a bunch of aliens. And they didn't look anything like me."

Dad nodded solemnly. "If you did, I wouldn't expect them to look like you," he said. "Because you are the last of your kind. The last survivor of your people."

"You are The One," Mom said, her voice trembling.

The One?

That's what Rikki and the others were talking

about in the darkroom. They said they had to find The One.

My head spun. "I—I don't understand," I said weakly. I gazed at my parents. "That means *you* are aliens, too?"

They shook their heads. "No. We found you, Ben," Mom answered. She came over and wrapped her arms around me. "Oh, Ben," she sighed. "Come with Dad and me. We can show you everything now. It's time you knew the whole story."

My legs were trembling as they led me upstairs. "Where are we going?" I asked.

"To the attic," Dad replied. "We can't hide this from you any longer."

Dad unlocked the door. We stepped inside the attic.

Then Mom opened the closet door. She reached in. A warm blue glow spread across the room.

The glow brightened as Mom pulled out a square thing about a foot tall and a foot wide.

I stared at it in amazement. It was some kind of screen, like a TV screen. Only it held a holographic image.

It showed three people—a male, a female, and a baby. They looked almost exactly like humans, but something was different about them.

They all had curly coarse brown hair. Their faces looked so much like mine. And then I realized what was weird about them.

They had *no ears*. And they all wore short tops over stomachs that had *no belly buttons*.

"I'll never forget the night we found you," Mom began.

"It was twelve years ago. I saw a weird light in the sky," Dad told me. "Like a pale blue glow."

"It was so close, and getting closer," Mom added. "We walked into the woods, following the light."

"We came to a clearing. I couldn't believe my eyes," Dad said. "I thought I was dreaming."

"A clearing?" I said. "In the woods behind our house?"

Mom nodded. "There was a huge spaceship. It was shaped like an eight. The ship was so hot it burned a mark on the grass. Sometimes I wonder if the mark is still there.

"We were so terrified at first, we ran away," Mom said. "But then we were curious. We went back into the woods. But the spaceship was gone."

"It had left that big mark in the grass," Dad said. "And lying right in the middle of the mark we saw something small. Something alive."

"That's when we found you, lying there in the grass," Mom said. "You were so cute! And so helpless!"

"Your mother picked you up and that was that," Dad said. "It was love at first sight. We were crazy about you. We wanted you to be our son."

"You mean you found me in the woods?" I asked. "But what made you think I was an alien?"

"This hologram," Mom explained. She pressed a button on the frame of it. The people inside the picture began to move.

"Please take care of our child," the woman in the picture begged. "He is the last of our race still alive. If he dies, our people will be extinct."

"He is The One," the man said. "The aliens who destroyed our planet will come after him one day. He is The One to defeat them. Our last chance . . . our one hope."

The figures stopped moving. I stared at the baby in the picture. "Is that . . . me?"

Mom nodded. "And those are your real parents."

"But what happened to me? I don't have any ears in that picture."

Mom and Dad exchanged glances. "That's right," Mom said. "When we found you, you had a hole on each side of your head."

I touched my ears. It had never occurred to me there was anything strange about them.

"We had a surgeon work on you secretly," Dad explained. "He gave you ears to cover the holes in your head. I always thought he did a great job."

"And what about my outie belly button?" I said, staring at the picture. "Did that grow in later?"

Mom shook her head. "We had the surgeon add that, too. I don't know why he gave you an outie. I guess it was easier to make than an innie."

I stared at the picture again. "So this is why you've been acting so mysterious and strange," I said. "That night you went out and you wouldn't tell us where you went. Where did you go? Why were you so late?"

"We're sorry if we frightened you," Dad said. "We just went for a drive. We sat in the car, talking about you. We were trying to decide what to do. We weren't sure if we should tell you where you came from."

"It was so hard for us," Mom added. "We've wanted so much for you to be a normal human boy. We knew that as soon as you found out you were an alien, you could never be normal again."

I laughed. "You were being so weird, I thought *you* were the aliens," I said.

I sat back in my chair, letting this new information sink in. It was still so hard to believe. I was an alien!

"What about Will?" I asked. "Is he an alien, too?"

"No," Mom replied. "He's our own, human child. He was born soon after we found you."

It *figured* Will would get to be the human child.

"But we love you just as much as we love Will," Mom insisted.

I was still in shock. So much was happening at once.

"We hoped you'd never have to know the truth," Dad told me. "But as you grew older, you became more and more obsessed with aliens. Without realizing it, you were searching for your roots. For your true identity."

"Does Will know about me?" I asked them.

Dad shook his head. "We've never told him anything. If you want him to know, it's up to you to tell him. We'll never say a word to him unless you ask us to."

It wasn't hard to imagine the kind of teasing I'd get from Will if he knew I was an alien. "Don't tell him," I said. "I don't want him to know."

Mom returned the hologram screen to the closet. "I suppose it's best to keep this hidden away," she said. "But if you ever want to come up and look at it, just let us know."

They each kissed me. Then we made our way downstairs.

I'm an alien, I thought. An alien!

It explained so much. Like why I felt such a jolt when I stepped inside that figure eight in the woods, and Summer and Jeff felt nothing.

I trudged to my room, feeling weary and dazed. My mind raced with a million weird thoughts.

I'm The One, I realized. I heard my true father say it.

I'm The One chosen from all the rest of my people

to battle the aliens who have come to Earth.

But how? What can I do against so many of them?

I lay on my bed and closed my eyes, thinking hard. Those egg-shaped aliens didn't seem to recognize me. The one inside me was sending his brain waves to me. He never once suspected that I wasn't human.

Yes, that's it. I'm not human, I realized.

The egg alien inside me must have died—because I'm not human!

Suddenly, I pictured the leader. The biggest, ugliest, most powerful alien.

What had I overheard about that big alien? They need the leader to survive—or they'd all die.

Maybe there's a way to defeat him, I thought. If I can do that, I can defeat them all.

But how?

My head swirled with crazy thoughts. I couldn't sleep, but tossed and turned in a strange half-dream state, my mind racing.

Rikki, Ms. Crenshaw, and the others were going to force all the kids at school to swallow those aliens. The aliens would live in their bodies forever.

Tomorrow . . . tomorrow . . .

They planned to carry out their plan tomorrow.

But how? How were they going to do it?

How would they force each kid, one by one, to swallow an alien?

Think, I instructed myself. Think, Ben. What is special about tomorrow?

"Oh!" I sat up in bed with a cry. I knew! Suddenly, I knew exactly what they planned to do!

"Ben, change your shirt," Mom said the next morning. "You're having your school picture taken today. Don't you want to look nice?"

Actually, looking nice was about the last thing on my mind. But I dutifully went upstairs and changed into a white button-down shirt.

"That's better," Mom said. She smoothed my hair over my ears. I suddenly realized that she'd done that all my life—smoothed my hair over my ears, I mean. And now I understood why.

"Ben doesn't have time to get his picture taken," Will teased. "He's too busy hunting aliens. He has to hunt for them at all times!"

I considered offering Will up as a sacrifice to the

127

egg-shaped aliens. They'd take over his personality. I thought it would be an improvement.

Then I shuddered. That could really happen, I realized. That could happen today.

At school, the kids looked extra nice. I could tell that their parents had made them dress a little neater than usual. Some of the girls looked as if they had their hair curled or straightened just for today. School Picture Day.

I felt so tense, I thought I might burst. I wanted to run down the halls shouting, "Go home! Go home! You're not safe here today!"

But instead, I found Ms. Crenshaw in the photo room. And I volunteered to help her with the school photos.

"Thank you, Ben," she said with a smile. She winked at me. She believed I still had the alien inside, controlling me. She believed I wanted to help her with her evil plan.

When photo time came, I headed for the gym, where the pictures would be taken.

Kids were lined up along the gym wall, waiting their turn. A few teachers hung around on the sidelines, making sure everything stayed under control.

Ms. Crenshaw had set up a curtain as a backdrop. Each kid was supposed to go behind the curtain.

Summer waved to me when she saw me. She was acting as Ms. Crenshaw's assistant. Rikki stood near the velvet curtain, ushering kids inside when it was their turn.

I stepped into the photo area. Ms. Crenshaw and Summer were setting it up.

Against the wall, I saw a tall stack of cages covered with a sheet. I knew what was under that sheet, what sat inside those cages.

The aliens.

"I think Ben will be a big help to us—now," Ms. Crenshaw said to Summer.

"Uh, yes," I replied. "I'll do whatever I can for the mission."

"Okay, Summer," Ms. Crenshaw said. "We're ready for the first host body. I mean, student."

Summer nodded at me. I went around to the other side of the curtain, where the kids stood in line. They were mostly from my class.

Summer poked her head around the curtain. "Go ahead, Ben," she said. "We're ready."

I had to go along with it. What else could I do? If I resisted, Summer would know that I was no longer an alien host. And then I'd have no chance to save the others.

The first kid in line happened to be Dennis Corcoran. I pointed to him. "You're up," I said.

Dennis's wavy hair had been wetted down and

combed flat, probably by his mother. Even though I didn't like Dennis, it made me sad to think about what was going to happen to him behind the curtain.

Dennis walked around the curtain. He nodded at Ms. Crenshaw, who stood behind the big camera on a tripod.

"Smile," Ms. Crenshaw said. "And open wide."

Dennis said, "Cheese." Then Rikki and Summer grabbed him. Rikki held him down while Summer opened his mouth and shoved a furry alien down his throat.

I cringed as I watched Dennis struggle. He tried to cry out, but his voice was muffled by the alien.

After a few seconds, he swallowed it.

He was now an alien host. And I was too late to save him.

Could I save the others?

What could I do?

Ms. Crenshaw snapped Dennis's picture. He stared blankly at the camera. The flash went off, blinding me for a moment.

Then Ms. Crenshaw called, "Next!" Dennis stepped out from behind the curtain, smiling as if nothing had happened.

A girl disappeared behind the curtain. I had to think quickly.

If I didn't do something, all the aliens would have human hosts. And I would be the only kid left in school who wasn't possessed.

One after another, the kids stepped behind the curtain. They had no idea what horror lay behind it.

No idea what was about to happen to them.

Summer stuffed an alien body down each throat. Ms. Crenshaw snapped a picture.

It was as if she were recording the first moment of their new lives. They were no longer human kids. Now they were just bodies, houses for aliens.

This can't go on, I thought. I racked my brain. Do something! Do something!

If only Rikki would stuff those aliens down *my* throat, I thought. Then they'd all die, just like the first one.

Yes!

Yes!

I finally had an idea.

I turned to the aliens' cages covered by a sheet. Was the leader in there?

I knew he had to be. The aliens couldn't go far without their leader.

I crossed over to the cages and peeked under the sheet. There he was. The biggest of the egg-shaped aliens, pulsing with energy.

Keeping the other aliens alive.

I knew what I had to do.

But I stopped in panic. The leader was more powerful than the others. A lot more powerful.

I remembered how the alien had fought inside my body. How I'd felt as if I were going to die.

What if the leader fought even harder? What if he

beat me—and survived inside me?

It's a risk I'll have to take, I realized. I'm The One. The One to defeat these aliens.

I opened the door to the leader's cage.

"Ben, get away from there!" Rikki scolded. She tried to pull me away from the cages. "What are you doing?"

I reached into the leader's cage and snatched him out. Rikki and Summer rushed at me.

"Put him down!" Rikki ordered. "Put him down!"

They tried to grab me, but I dodged away from them.

I opened my mouth as wide as I could.

"Ben, no!" Rikki screamed.

I froze. I gazed at the big hairy creature. Thick blue mucus dripped from its body onto my hands, my arms.

Could I do it? Could I swallow the disgusting thing?

Yes. I stuffed the leader into my mouth. With a huge push I shoved him down my throat.

Gagging, choking, my mouth tingling with fur, I swallowed him.

I felt the alien body sink heavily into my stomach.

He felt different from the other alien. Bigger and stronger.

He wriggled and squirmed inside me. He's fighting me, I realized. He must sense that I'm not human.

Rikki and Summer grabbed me by the arms and shook me. "What are you doing? Why did you do that? Are you crazy?"

"I—*ugh!*" I grunted. The leader was fighting me

hard, raging in fury. I doubled over, crying out in pain.

Rikki and Summer held on to me tightly. They glared at me angrily.

Slowly, their expressions changed. Their faces went blank.

Their hands slipped off me. I saw their knees buckle.

With loud groans, they both collapsed to the floor.

In the gym, I saw the other kids fall, too. They dropped to the floor, twitching, rolling, bouncing.

"People! Everyone!" one of the teachers shouted. "Stop fooling around! What's the matter with you?"

But the kids' bodies jerked on the floor as they screamed in pain.

Inside me, I felt the leader fighting. He seemed to be bouncing off the sides of my stomach.

I screamed in agony as I felt his teeth digging into my insides. Was he trying to chew his way out of me?

I dropped to my knees on the gym floor, clutching my stomach.

"Ben!" a teacher cried, bending over me. "What is it?"

I shook my head. I couldn't speak. The pain was too intense.

"Somebody call an ambulance!" the teacher shouted. "Hurry!"

Through the pain, I began to hear the leader's voice inside my head.

"You can't beat me," he said. *"I am all-powerful. I will sap the strength out of you."*

"You can't kill me. I'm going to kill you first."

Another stab of pain shot through my body. I could hear the other kids around me screaming, as if from a distance, as if in a dream.

They were all fading, fading away. I could feel myself fading, too. I couldn't stand the pain much longer.

I can't let him win, I thought. I struggled to hold on, to fight him. But I could feel him growing stronger, angrier. His rage made him powerful.

I struggled to my feet.

But I was too weak to stand.

And the pain . . . the pain . . .

I dropped back to the floor.

I've lost, I realized.

I've let everyone down. I've lost . . .

"You don't know?" I wailed. "You're still aliens?"

Summer broke into a grin. "We're teasing you, Ben. We wouldn't forget the gross thing you did with that pea."

"It still makes me sick to my stomach," Jeff said.

"I'm sorry about all the things the aliens made us do to you," Summer said. "Really sorry. But you saved us! You saved us all! I don't know how to thank you."

"How did you do it?" Jeff asked. "What happened when you swallowed the leader? Why did he die? He was supposed to thrive inside a human body."

Summer stared at me. "Hey—that's right," she said. "How did you kill the leader?"

"Uh—um . . . well . . ." I stammered. What could I say? That the leader died because I'm not human? Because I'm an alien? Because I am The One?

No.

Maybe someday I'll want to tell people, I thought. Maybe someday I'll want to explore my alien roots. And tell the whole world who I really am.

But not now.

For now I just want to live a normal human life with my family and friends.

So what could I tell them? How could I explain it?

As they stared at me, waiting for an explanation, an idea popped into my head.

"The leader died because I'm not human," I told them. "You see, he died because I'm an alien from outer space, too!"

They both laughed.

Jeff rolled his eyes. "Yeah. For sure! Good one, Ben!"

"Very funny," Summer said, slapping me on the back. "So now you're an alien, too. Very funny. Ha-ha."

She slapped me on the back again.

And the three of us walked out of the gym, laughing at my crazy joke.

ABOUT THE AUTHOR

R.L. STINE says he has a great job. "My job is to give kids the CREEPS!" With his scary books, R.L. has terrified kids all over the world. He has sold over 300 million books, making him the best-selling children's author in history.

These days, R.L. is dishing out new frights in his series THE NIGHTMARE ROOM. When he isn't working, he likes to read old mysteries, watch *SpongeBob Squarepants* on TV, and take his dog, Nadine, for long walks around New York City, where he lives with his wife, Jane, and son, Matthew.